The sun was already low in the western sky when Jed pulled his Bronco to the side of the road.

Turning slightly in his seat, he put a hand on Caitlin's arm. "Do you mind if we stop here? I just wanted to be alone for a minute, to say goodbye."

"I know what you mean," Caitlin said, smiling.

"I also want to tell you how proud I am of you," Jed said in a low voice. "You were great today. And those kids loved you."

"Well, you were terrific, too," Caitlin said. She let out a small sigh and slipped her hand around his neck. "Jed, I love you so very much. You're everything I need. Everything I'll ever want. I couldn't stand it if we were ever separated again—like last summer."

"Let's just forget about last summer," he murmured. "Let's think about the future." He kissed her tenderly on the forehead. "Because, I promise, we're going to have the best future any two people ever had." He kissed her again, this time on the cheek. "We'll never let anything come between us again. You'll see—never."

He looked deep into her blue eyes. "And that's a promise I am going to keep."

Caitlin

TENDER PROMISES

Created by
Francine Pascal

Written by
Diana Gregory

BANTAM BOOKS
TORONTO · NEW YORK · LONDON · SYDNEY · AUCKLAND

RL 6, IL age 12 and up

TENDER PROMISES

A Bantam Book / November 1986

Conceived by Francine Pascal

Produced by Cloverdale Press Inc.

ISBN 0-553-25812-5

Bantam Books are published by Bantam Books, Inc. Its trademark, consisting of the words "Bantam Books" and the portrayal of a rooster, is Registered in U.S. Patent and Trademark Office and in other countries. Marca Registrada. Bantam Books, Inc., 666 Fifth Avenue, New York, New York 10103.

PRINTED IN THE UNITED STATES OF AMERICA

O   0 9 8 7 6 5 4 3 2 1

TENDER
PROMISES

1

Caitlin Ryan and her boyfriend, Jed Michaels, were standing on the stone terrace, looking out at the fireflies winking in the soft dusk that had settled down over the sweeping back lawn of the Ryan estate. A small dinner party given by Caitlin's grandmother, Regina Ryan, had just ended, and Jed and Caitlin had escaped to the quiet of the terrace.

Jed slipped his arms around Caitlin's waist and pulled her loosely back against him. "Happy?"

"Oh, Jed." Caitlin sighed contentedly. "That's the understatement of the year." She nestled her head against his shoulder. The rich blackness of her hair contrasted sharply with his white dinner jacket. "I just keep thinking about how great this summer is going to be." She turned her head and looked up into his rugged, handsome face. Her deep blue eyes appeared almost violet in the darkening light. "What makes it so wonderful is that we're going to be spending it together. Not like last summer." She moved

1

closer to him, as if to push the painful memory away. But she knew she would never be able to forget the incident that had kept them apart the summer before.

Almost two years before when she and Jed were in their junior year at Highgate Academy, Caitlin had been responsible for an accident that had temporarily crippled the dean's son. By the time Caitlin realized that the accident was her fault, another student had already been blamed for it and left school. Caitlin couldn't bring herself to tell anyone the truth. She thought she would be able to live with her guilt—that it would lessen as the days went by—but that hadn't happened. Caitlin's guilt had haunted her; she was always afraid someone would discover what she had inadvertently done. Finally Jed *had* found out, and he couldn't forgive her. He stayed away from Caitlin despite her attempts to make up for what she'd done. But eventually Caitlin had taken full responsibility for the accident, and Jed had admitted he couldn't live without her.

"I know, Caitlin." Jed's arm tightened momentarily as he, too, remembered the terrible parting. Then, taking his arm from around her waist, he gently turned her so that she was facing him. "But that's all in the past. And we've got the whole summer to look forward to." He smiled. "You know, when I first met you, I never would have dreamed that a society girl like Caitlin Ryan would organize a summer preschool program for miners' children."

"Well"—she looked up into Jed's incredible green eyes—"that was a long time ago." Lifting her hand, she lightly traced one finger from where his brown, wavy hair curled just above his ear, down along the strong, angular line of his jaw to the cleft in his chin. "I have changed a lot since then."

"Um-hum." Gently he captured her finger with his hand and kissed the tip. "Talk about understatement . . ." His voice drifted off into the still night air.

"But really, Jed," Caitlin said, her blue eyes sparkling, "I *am* excited about the project. I'm so glad Emily has agreed to help. And I can't believe Matt is going to help, too. He's actually giving us four weeks of his time."

"He didn't have much choice," Jed answered, laughing. "He owed me."

"Owed you?" Caitlin asked, a puzzled expression crossing her face. "How come?"

"Well, he wasn't exactly the neatest roommate in the world. He was always taking my clean socks and giving them back dirty. Then there was the time he spilled Coke all over my term paper, and—"

"Stop!" Caitlin laughed, too. "I get the idea. Whatever his *real* reasons are, I'm glad he'll be with us. He's so good at putting together skits and stuff like that. We need him."

Jed nodded. "And Emily's great, too. She's a natural around kids."

"Oh, don't I know it. And the best part of her being involved is you'll be able to live with her

3

and her family. I know they're your aunt and uncle, but they didn't have to take you in. It was awfully nice of them to ask you."

"It was." Jed's green eyes teased. "But the very best part of everything is living close to you."

"Oh, really?" Caitlin teased back. "Well, I hope—"

Caitlin was interrupted by a silvery peal of laughter coming from an open set of French doors farther down the terrace. Mrs. Regina Ryan was in the library with her dinner guest. They had gone there to discuss business.

"Come on, Jed," Caitlin said. "Let's take a walk to the stables. It's more private there, and I want to say good night to Duster, anyway. I'm not sure he's used to being back home yet. After all, it's only been a couple of days." Caitlin, an expert rider, had boarded her favorite horse at Highgate Academy.

"Sounds good to me," Jed agreed. He took Caitlin's hand, and the two of them started to walk across the lawn. Caitlin mentioned the man who had been Mrs. Ryan's dinner guest and to whom she was now talking in the library. "Grandmother's been interviewing a lot of lawyers to take over as Ryan Mining's attorney. That Mr. Constable is one of the candidates. What did you think of him?"

"I have no idea if he's a good attorney," Jed replied. "But he seems nice enough. Why?"

"I liked him, too," she said in a thoughtful tone. "He's a lot better than some of the others.

4

There's one who I really don't like." She shivered involuntarily at the thought of him. "And I'm afraid she'll choose him."

"Why don't you like him?" Jed had noticed her shiver. "Hey, are you cold?"

"No." Caitlin shook her head. "It's just thinking about that other lawyer—Colin Wollman. He keeps coming over to the house, and every time I see him I get a creepy feeling."

"What's wrong with him?"

Caitlin shook her head. "I don't honestly know. He's certainly good-looking." She shrugged.

"Maybe I should be jealous."

"Hardly!" Caitlin shot Jed a serious look. "Aside from the fact that he gives me the creeps, he's a little old for me. He's somewhere in his forties."

"Well, don't worry about him," Jed advised. "You said she's still interviewing. That probably means she's decided she doesn't like him, either."

"I hope so. Once my grandmother makes up her mind about something, or someone, she rarely changes it." Caitlin gave a small shake of her head, then turned and smiled at Jed. She still couldn't believe how handsome he was. "You're right, I'll try not to worry. But I do wish she'd hurry up and make up her mind. I'm tired of having to sit through these formal dinners every night. And having to dress every evening can get a little tiring, too."

"I don't know." Jed gave her an appreciative

look. A light breeze was blowing across the lawn, rippling Caitlin's yellow silk dress. It outlined her long, slim legs. "I think it's worth the trouble when you end up looking as gorgeous as you do right now."

"I'm glad you approve," Caitlin said, her eyes sparkling.

"Speaking of your grandmother," Jed said a few moments later, "I'm a little surprised that she's not putting up any argument about your coming to Montana with me for a month after our work with the preschool project is over."

"What do you mean?"

"Well, just that I had the feeling that she didn't entirely approve of me, or of anyone who was born in the West. I always thought that, as far as she was concerned, I was nothing but an ignorant cowboy from Montana."

"She's over that now, Jed. You know that. I admit that when she first met you, she did have reservations about you. But you've more than proven yourself. Anyone who knows horses as well as you do impresses her. Besides"—she waved her arm to take in the grounds of the estate—"your father's ranch must be thirty times the size of Ryan Acres. And you're hardly poor, Jed. That alone would earn her respect."

"I know she'd like me a lot better if she thought that this summer would be the last she'd see of me." Jed turned to look at Caitlin. "Am I wrong, or was tonight at dinner the first she'd heard that we'd be at Carleton Hill together this fall? She looked surprised when I mentioned it."

"I'm sure I must have said something about it before," Caitlin lied. She knew she hadn't told her grandmother that Jed would be going to the same university that she was. Caitlin had put off saying anything because she knew her grandmother wouldn't be entirely pleased. "Oh, she was probably just distracted," Caitlin said, reassuring Jed and squeezing his hand for emphasis.

They had passed the tennis court and pool and were approaching the large colonial-style stable. Jeff, the man who ran the stable, was just coming through the wide, arched doorway.

"Hello, Jeff," she called.

"Good evening, Miss Ryan," he greeted her in return, lifting his cap politely. "Come to visit Duster?"

"Yes. I thought I'd let him know I haven't deserted him."

"I'm sure he wouldn't think a thing like that, Miss Ryan." Jeff chuckled warmly. Lifting his cap again, he said, "Well, I was just leaving. Do you need me for anything before I go?"

"No," Caitlin said. "But thanks. You have a good evening."

"Same to yourself. And to you, too, sir," he said, this time merely touching the brim of his cap with one finger.

Entering the barn, Caitlin made a quick stop at the feed room. She grabbed a couple of carrots from the metal bin.

"I know. I know," she said before Jed could

7

say anything. "I spoil Duster terribly. But it's only because I love him. I can't help it."

Jed smiled. "Tell me," he said, raising and lowering his eyebrows playfully, "does that mean I can count on you spoiling me, too?"

Quickly he dodged away from Caitlin as she brandished one of the carrots at him. "Absolutely not!" she said, trying to sound serious. Coming to a standstill, she put one hand on her hip. "I only spoil horses." With a flip of her head, she turned down the aisle again. Halfway to Duster's stall, she stopped and looked impishly over her shoulder. "I never spoil tall, handsome men who should be spoiling me instead." Then she looked toward Duster again. "Isn't that right, big boy?" she asked her horse. Duster nickered in response.

She was offering Duster a carrot, holding it out to him on the flat of her palm, when Jed came up and leaned against the top edge of the stall door.

Duster arched his shining black neck and nibbled softly at the treat. Then he took it gently into his mouth. As Caitlin broke off another piece to offer him, she tipped her head and looked at Jed through thick, dark lashes. "Would you like to?" she asked teasingly.

"What? Spoil you?" Taking in the lovely picture of the two of them, the sleek, black horse and the beautiful girl he loved, he grinned easily. "Well, maybe. But only a little."

"I'll remember you said that." Caitlin gave Duster the rest of the carrots and a final pat.

"You just wait until I get you out to Montana," Jed promised. "Then you'll see what we call real western hospitality."

"Ummm." Caitlin closed her eyes, and smiled softly. "I can hardly wait."

"Perhaps I shouldn't make you wait, after all. Maybe I should give you a small sample now." With that, he put both arms around her and pulled her close. Before she could open her eyes, he gently kissed one eyelid and then the other. Then he kissed the tip of her nose and finally her mouth. Caitlin shivered—this time with happiness.

2

As Caitlin drove her red 280ZX along the interstate highway, she smiled to herself. It was a
perfectly glorious summer day, and she was
headed for the small private hospital where her
father, Dr. Gordon Westlake, was director. They
had a date for lunch, and she was looking
forward to their time together.

Wanting everything about the luncheon date
to be absolutely perfect, she had tried on several
outfits before settling on the white, pleated linen
slacks and deep blue silk blouse. The color of the
blouse complimented her new sapphire earrings. Raising a hand, she touched one. They
had been a present from her father. "A little
surprise," he had said simply as he handed her
the tiny box wrapped in silver paper.

The present had touched her deeply. It wasn't
because the sapphires had been expensive, although they were. Caitlin loved the earrings
because they were a token of her father's love—a
love she had found only a few months earlier.
Until a year ago Dr. Westlake had not even

known he had a daughter. He had been unofficially engaged to Regina Ryan's daughter, Laura, much to Mrs. Ryan's dismay. She had taken her daughter to Europe, where Laura discovered she was pregnant. Caitlin's mother had died in childbirth, and Caitlin had been led to believe that her father had deserted her immediately afterward. But they had each other now. And they were making up for all the years they'd lost.

The cassette she had been playing ended, and Caitlin replaced it with another one. As the song floated out of the speakers, she thought about how she was going to approach the subject with her father—that she wanted to use his last name, Westlake, when she went to Rock Ridge to work with the miners' children.

She had absolutely no worries that her father would object. Just the opposite—she was afraid that he might take it the wrong way. Caitlin didn't want him to think that she was weakening in favor of his request to change her last name to his.

He had asked her several times over the past months if she would do it. "After all, Caitlin," he told her each time they were together, "Westlake is your rightful name." He had even asked her to move in with him.

But, although the thought of using his name and moving in with him appealed to her, she had had to refuse. She couldn't bring herself to do something that might hurt her grandmother so deeply. Her grandmother had, after all, raised her. She had sent her to the best schools, taken her on the most exotic vacations, and made sure she always had the best of everything. The only thing Regina Ryan had not given freely to Caitlin was her love. But Caitlin now knew she had held back her love out of the bitterness she'd felt when her only daughter had died in childbirth. But more than any of those things—and Caitlin frowned at the thought—her grandmother wasn't as strong as usual lately. She was sick more often, and Caitlin was reminded that Regina Ryan was getting older. She could neither leave her nor change her name now.

Caitlin pulled off the interstate and slowed down to turn into the entrance of Meadow Valley Hospital. As she rounded the drive, she could see her father waiting for her. His tall, athletic figure looked poised and confident beneath the front portico of the modern brick building. Whenever she saw him, Caitlin always felt a little thrill of pride that this handsome man was, indeed, her father. As she pulled up and braked to a stop, she noticed how especially good-looking he appeared that day. He was dressed in beige slacks, a dark blue raw silk sport jacket, and a hunter green shirt that set off his dark good looks, which Caitlin had inherited.

"Hello!" she called, raising her hand to wave. "I hope I'm not too late."

"Not late at all," he said, walking quickly to the side of the car, opening the door, and sliding in. "I left my office a little early so no one would find me and make me late." He leaned over and gave her a fatherly kiss on the cheek. "You look positively radiant today. Are those the earrings I gave you?"

"Yes." She kissed his cheek in return. "And you know how much I love them, don't you?"

"I do, and I'm glad." He smiled and buckled his seat belt.

"So, where are we going for lunch?" she asked happily, putting the car into first gear.

Dr. Westlake gave her directions, and minutes later they were back on the interstate, heading toward Martinsburg. "I think you're going to like the restaurant I've picked, Caitlin. It's new, and they serve the best Italian food I've ever tasted. I know how much you love good Italian food."

"Oh, yes. I do." Caitlin nodded. "It's strange that we have so many similar tastes." She glanced over at him briefly. "Do you think that it could possibly be hereditary?"

Dr. Westlake let out a hearty laugh. "Well, I'm not sure. It's possible."

As they came into the outskirts of town, Dr. Westlake directed her toward a small side street where a line of pre-Civil War buildings had been restored and converted into little shops and restaurants.

The restaurant was located on the ground floor of one of those buildings. It was a tiny place, with room for only half a dozen tables, which were laid with blue- and white-checkered cloths and set with pewter plate holders and bowls of fresh white flowers. A plump, smiling woman led them to a table by the window. As they sat down, she gave them menus and left.

It took only moments for Caitlin to decide what she would have. Dr. Westlake gave the order to the waiter, who had appeared a moment earlier with glasses of ice water for them.

"Now," her father said as he spread his napkin over his lap. "What shall we talk about?" His eyes twinkled. "Perhaps you'd like to hear about my most recent patients and all of their various complications? Or, perhaps"—he leaned slightly forward, and his eyes looked warmly into hers—"you would rather just start right out and tell me why you wanted to have lunch today." As she started to protest, he held up a hand to stop her. "Oh, I know you enjoy having lunch with me *anytime*. But I get the feeling there's something special about today. And I'm wondering, would it have anything to do with this project you're about to embark on—what's it called?"

"Sometimes you're just too smart," Caitlin said, then grinned. "The project is called Project Acorn. Jed's cousin Emily came up with the name."

"Acorn is very appropriate," Dr. Westlake agreed. "It gives the impression that you will be helping the kids grow."

"Yes." Caitlin smiled. "That's why we liked it. We wanted to give the kids in Rock Ridge an opportunity to build basic skills—and have fun, too, of course."

She paused as the waiter placed their orders in front of them. Dr. Westlake had ordered linguini with clam sauce, while Caitlin had ordered a fluffy seafood frittata.

"Anyway," she went on, after tasting her omelet and stating that it was perfectly delicious, "the basic idea is pretty simple. Project Acorn is basically a play group for younger children. We'll teach them games and crafts, and maybe their letters and numbers, stuff like that. It'll give working mothers a place to leave their kids and know they're safe. And it will give mothers who stay at home some time to themselves."

"I'm fairly certain," Dr. Westlake commented, "that since you helped organize the project, it isn't so simple as just playing games a few hours a day. Am I right?"

"Well, we *have* put a lot of work into it. I did some research and found out that a lot of these mountain people have colorful backgrounds to draw on. Did you know that many of them are descendants of people who came over here from England and Scotland a couple of hundred years ago? They still sing folk songs that have to do with kings and queens and battles that took place over there."

"No, quite honestly, I didn't," he said. "I grew up in the mountains, but we weren't miners. I guess I never thought much about it before."

"I hadn't, either," Caitlin agreed. "So what we've done is to organize the games and activities around this background. Instead of bringing in our customs, I thought it would be better to give the children a chance to show off what they know about their own heritage—to have pride in it. And, perhaps, to learn even more." She took a sip of the mineral water that had been served with her meal. "What I'm finding that's so great is that all of us are learning as well."

"That makes the name Acorn even more meaningful."

"I think so," Caitlin agreed.

"I really like that." Dr. Westlake spun some more linguini around his fork before continuing. "Tell me, just how did you manage to set all of this up?"

"I didn't do it myself," she explained. "In fact, I couldn't even go out there because of school. Mrs. Van Allen, the teacher at Highgate who acted as our sponsor, took care of all the formalities and details. As you know, Jed and I will only be there for a month. But Mrs. Van Allen is coordinating the project for the whole summer. Anyway, she went to Rock Ridge and talked to the people there. But I did speak to one of the mothers on the phone a few times—Lola Butler. She's sort of the spokesperson for the younger women. Anyway, it was from talking to her, and finding out what the children were like, that I decided to use the background idea."

"Sounds very well organized." Taking a last bite, he put down his fork and pushed his plate slightly to one side. "I'm very proud of you for doing all of this."

16

"Thanks. Coming from you, that means a lot."

"And *you* mean a lot to me," he answered gently. "So, when do you start?"

"On Monday. I wish we'd had time to go there and set up and look around, but with graduation and all, we were swamped. But Mrs. Van Allen has spent the last few days there." She paused, then looked him straight in the eye. "And now I want to ask you something."

"Ahhh." Dr. Westlake nodded slowly. "At last, the real reason for my getting to spend some time with you. So what's on your mind?"

"I want to know if you have any objections to my using the name Westlake when I go to Rock Ridge. In fact," she hurried on, "that woman I talked to on the phone—Lola Butler—already thinks that's my name."

"You know I don't mind a bit, but may I ask why?"

"Well, I'm afraid that if I go there using the name Ryan, it'll scare some people away. They'll assume that I'm there to represent Ryan Mining, and since most of them work for Grandmother, that's the last thing I want. I want to be able to gain their confidence. Once I do that, then I'll be able to tell them who I am."

"I see." Dr. Westlake was thoughtful. "Well, of course I don't have any objections to your using the Westlake name." A smile touched his lips. "You know I'd love to have you take it permanently." The smile turned to a look of concern. "Does your grandmother know of your plan?"

"No. And I don't want her to ever find out. I don't think she'd understand my reasons."

"I'm sure she wouldn't." Dr. Westlake's expression made it obvious that he thought Regina Ryan could never understand. "But it seems to me that you're playing a dangerous game with this deception. You've not only got the people of Rock Ridge but also your grandmother to hide from. I hope you gain their confidence quickly because it will be hard to keep it a secret."

"I'm going to try," Caitlin said sincerely. "With Grandmother—" Caitlin made a face, not needing to end the sentence.

"Well then, let's hope Regina Ryan never finds out." Dr. Westlake smiled conspiratorially as he put his hand across the table and took hers, squeezing it gently. "As I said, I'm very, very proud of you."

Suddenly he glanced at his watch. "It's later than I thought. I've got to go—I have rounds this afternoon."

He reached into his pocket for his wallet, then raised his hand to signal the waiter that he was ready for the check. Looking back at Caitlin, he said, "Time goes by so quickly when I'm with you. I just wish we had more of it."

"I do, too, Father," Caitlin replied in a soft voice. "I do, too."

3

Caitlin and her grandmother were breakfasting on the terrace the following morning. Caitlin knew her grandmother would take advantage of their time together to ask her how her lunch with her father had gone. And she wouldn't enjoy being pumped.

"So, tell me, dear, what did you and your father talk about?" Mrs. Ryan smiled at Caitlin, her silver spoon poised just above the dish of chilled grapefruit segments on the table before her.

"Oh, nothing special, Grandmother," Caitlin replied. "You know—just the usual things."

"Well, but surely you can remember something of what the two of you discussed."

However pleasant and casual her grandmother's probing was superficially, Caitlin felt as though she were being grilled by the FBI. Her grandmother was always on guard to come up with any information that she could use against Dr. Westlake—anything to justify her keeping the truth from Caitlin for so long. But the truth had come out: Gordon Westlake hadn't deserted his daughter—he hadn't even known he had a daughter. He had wanted to marry Laura Ryan, but her mother was against the relationship. To her, Gordon Westlake was just a poor medical student—hardly adequate for a Ryan. She had lied to Laura, saying horrible things about Dr. Westlake. Mrs Ryan had whisked her daughter to Europe, and only after they'd arrived had Laura Ryan discovered that she was pregnant. Later, when Laura died giving birth to Caitlin, Regina Ryan had been angry and bitter enough to blame Dr. Westlake for her daughter's death. She came to hate him so much that she vowed she would never tell him about his child.

Then, the previous fall, Caitlin had been involved in a serious accident. Both her father and grandmother had feared for her life. In an emotional confrontation, Dr. Westlake had insisted that Mrs. Ryan finally tell Caitlin the truth, and she had relented. Because they both loved Caitlin, they had formed a truce. But it was an uneasy truce since they each resented having to share Caitlin's love. Caitlin continued to hope that their relationship would eventually change.

"What about your project in Rock Ridge?" Mrs. Ryan broke the small moment of silence, and then she reached for the silver coffeepot to refill her cup. "Surely you must have talked about that. Being as conscientious a doctor as he is, I'm certain he's brimming over with humanitarian feelings."

"Yes. He approved." Caitlin spooned up a

grapefruit segment, then put it down with a little plop. Almost defiantly she said, "And he likes the name, Project Acorn. He thinks it's quite fitting."

"Humph! He would." Mrs. Ryan raised a hand to summon the maid, who was waiting close by. "That's not to say that I don't believe in good works. I most certainly do. It's only that I don't approve of doing volunteer work when you can give money instead. It is money that people need and want the most—not volunteers."

Caitlin didn't bother replying, having heard the same argument many times before. Instead, she sat quietly, hoping that her grandmother would say no more about her father.

The maid cleared away the fruit dishes and replaced them with hand-painted blue-and-white porcelain cups containing soft-boiled eggs. Then she put a plate of toast points and a crystal divided dish holding an assortment of English jams and marmalade on the table.

When the maid left, Mrs. Ryan picked up her spoon and lightly tapped the top of the shell on the soft-boiled egg to break it open. "Actually, I don't think I would have allowed you to become involved with the project if it hadn't been for some advice given to me by a person I consider very wise. He convinced me that the project was an excellent image builder for Ryan Mining." She paused to spoon out some of her egg and eat it with a bit of toast.

Caitlin's mind was racing, trying to think of

who her grandmother could possibly mean. But she couldn't think of anyone. She was about to ask who it was when her grandmother told her.

"You remember Mr. Wollman, don't you, Caitlin?" Mrs. Ryan's eyes came alive as she spoke his name. "He's such an intelligent and shrewd gentleman, so knowledgeable in so many areas—art, the theater, as well as business and law. That's why I've decided to offer him the position of attorney for Ryan Mining." She smiled at Caitlin.

But Caitlin could only stare back. Finally she found her voice. "Colin Wollman?"

"That's right, dear." Mrs. Ryan smiled again. "I'm confident he'll do an excellent job for us. And I also hope he'll be with the company for many years to come. I have a luncheon date with him at the country club today. I want to discuss Ryan Mining's legal requirements and his new position. I'm also going to tell him that I'm planning a party to introduce him to some of my friends. But since our date isn't until noon and I have the morning free, I thought you and I might play a few sets of tennis. I know we could play right here, but I do so love the grass courts at the club. And it will give us some time together, especially since you'll be so wrapped up in this little project of yours for the next four weeks. Then off to Montana for a month."

"I'd love to join you for tennis, Grandmother," Caitlin answered automatically. She was still stunned by the news that, of all the men her grandmother had interviewed for the job of

company attorney, she had picked the only one
Caitlin disliked.

Mrs. Ryan rose from her chair, placing her
napkin to the left of her plate. "Good," she said
in a businesslike tone. "Oh, I think it would be
better if you took your car. I'll want Rollins and
the Bentley for the remainder of the day. I'll see
you on the grass courts at ten—a court has
already been reserved for us." Barely waiting for
Caitlin's nod of agreement, she went through
the french doors and into the house, the heels of
her pumps clicking on the flagstones as she
went.

Caitlin watched her leave and then stared
down at her untouched breakfast. She was not
hungry, but she knew she'd need her energy if
she was to play well against her grandmother.
The egg had gotten cold, so she pushed it aside.
Picking up a piece of toast, she nibbled on it. She
drank a sip of cold coffee to wash it down.

At 9:45 sharp Caitlin drove through the entrance of the Mountain Gate Country Club. She
continued directly up to the imposing main
building, where she turned the 280ZX over to
the parking attendant.

Because she had come to the club only to play
tennis and wouldn't be going into the clubhouse
for anything, she had worn her tennis clothes.
She went straight through the lobby and out
onto the back terrace. From there she took the
winding path down past the clay courts to the

grass ones her grandmother preferred. With a sigh of relief, she sat down on the bench at the side of the court. Her grandmother wasn't there yet. Unzipping her bag, she took out her head- and wristbands and slipped them on. Then she popped open a can of tennis balls. Taking out two, she walked over to the backboard and began warming up. Mrs. Ryan arrived soon after that, and they took their places on the court.

An hour and a half later Caitlin began to tire in the muggy heat. She had been playing hard. Though Caitlin was by far the better athlete, her grandmother was playing extremely well, and the score stayed fairly even.

It was Caitlin's second serve; she had missed the first. Pausing to wipe the perspiration from her neck, she glanced across the net. She noticed with some satisfaction that her grandmother, also wilting in the humid heat, no longer looked as cool and elegant as she had when they had started.

Frowning slightly, Mrs. Ryan called with impatience, "What are you waiting for, Caitlin? Serve."

"I was just about to," Caitlin called back. With a weary sigh, she tossed the ball into the air and drove it forward. The ball sailed over the net.

"Out!" Mrs. Ryan called across the court. "My game and serve."

Caitlin gave a tired nod and moved, ready to receive. She watched as her grandmother walked over to retrieve a ball from the baseline. But as Mrs. Ryan bent to pick it up, she suddenly stumbled, going down on one knee.

"Grand—" Caitlin started to call out. But her voice caught in her throat as Mrs. Ryan's other knee buckled beneath her. The older woman tossed her racquet aside and put both hands out in front of her to prevent herself from falling. Caitlin heard the racquet hit the court surface with a soft thud. She raced across the court.

"Grandmother! Grandmother!" Caitlin said in a breathless, frightened voice when she reached Mrs. Ryan's side. "Are you all right?" Even as she asked the question, she could see how pale her grandmother was. She looked terrible.

"Can you stand? Here, let me help you over to the shade."

Frantically Caitlin looked around to see if there was anyone in sight. But they were the only people on the lower courts, and they were hidden from view by a large, flowering hedge. "Do you want me to go find a doctor?"

"No, no." Low and weak at first, Mrs. Ryan's voice gained strength, and a little color returned to her face. "Don't be absurd, Caitlin." She raised her head. "It was only the heat. I felt dizzy there for a second, that's all." Taking a breath, she started to get to her feet. "Oh—" she gasped, collapsing onto her hands and knees again. She closed her eyes. Then, with obvious effort, she opened them. Putting a hand on Caitlin's arm, she said, "Help me up, will you?"

Caitlin put her arm around her grandmother

25

and helped her to her feet. They walked slowly to a nearby bench in the shade. Mrs. Ryan sank gratefully onto the wooden seat. Not quite knowing what to do, Caitlin sat down beside her.

"I'm all right, Caitlin. Really, I am," Mrs. Ryan said a bit irritably. But she gave a heavy sigh and leaned back. Caitlin could tell the few steps they had walked had tired her grandmother. Her hand was on her grandmother's arm, and Caitlin could feel the older woman's slender body shaking. It worried her tremendously.

"Are you sure you don't want me to see if I can find a doctor?"

"No, Caitlin. I don't want a doctor." Mrs. Ryan shook her head firmly. "That's the last thing I want you to do. But you could get me some iced tea." She gestured toward her tennis bag. "There's some in the thermos over there."

Getting up, Caitlin quickly walked over to where the blue nylon bag sat against the fence. She found the thermos and brought it back. Opening it, she poured some tea into the cup that served as a top and held the cup out to her grandmother.

"That's much better," Mrs. Ryan said, after taking several sips.

But Caitlin was still worried. "I won't go for a doctor if you don't want me to. But I do think I should get one of the club attendants to help you back to the locker room. You should at least lie down for a minute."

"Nonsense!" Mrs. Ryan's voice was strong

and firm. "You will do no such thing." She sat up. "I'm perfectly all right. As I said, it was nothing but a momentary dizzy spell from the heat." She frowned at Caitlin. "In fact, you appear a little flushed yourself."

I feel a little flushed, Caitlin thought to herself. But her grandmother had been *pale* in spite of the heat.

"But, Grandmother," Caitlin persisted, "you have to start being more careful. After all, you're not as young—"

"I am not some sick old woman, Caitlin. In fact, I had my semiannual checkup only last month, and Dr. Carter assures me I'm in excellent health."

"But—" Caitlin gave up. Her grandmother could be so stubborn when she wanted to.

"But I have had enough tennis for today." She glanced at her watch. "I should be going in to change for lunch, anyway." This time she stood on her own. And as Caitlin went to take her arm to assist her, she shook it off. "Don't treat me as though I were an invalid, Caitlin! If you would carry my bag and racquet for me, I can walk back without further help."

Caitlin walked her grandmother to the women's locker room, where she was dismissed. Her grandmother waved her away, saying, "Go along, now. As I said, I have a business lunch, and you'd only be in the way. I'm certain you have other things planned for this afternoon." Her words had been almost curt, but Mrs. Ryan had softened them with a smile. Caitlin knew that her grandmother's harsh words had only been her way of proving her strength—to both of them.

Caitlin said goodbye and left. But, instead of going home, Caitlin went back out to the terrace. She sat down at one of the umbrella-shaded tables and ordered a glass of sparkling water with a twist of lime. Then she waited, looking through the huge picture windows into the lobby, for her grandmother to appear. Caitlin wanted to make sure she was really all right.

Half an hour later, Caitlin saw her grandmother enter the lobby from the direction of the locker room. Looking cool and elegant in a jade green linen suit, Mrs. Ryan walked briskly across the plush carpet. Her silver hair was swept back from her patrician face. She looked so strong and in control that Caitlin almost wondered if she had imagined the incident on the tennis court.

Smiling in relief, Caitlin got up to leave. But her smile froze as she saw her grandmother's luncheon companion walk across the lobby to greet her, his hands reaching out to take hers. It was Colin Wollman. Caitlin knew then that he would be playing a large part in her grandmother's life. And that meant he would play a large part in her life, too.

4

On Monday morning Caitlin heard Jed come roaring up the drive in his new Bronco. He'd bought the four-wheel drive vehicle because the roads near Rock Ridge were mostly unpaved. By the time he pulled up in front of the wide steps leading to the front door, she was already halfway down them. A girl with short, dark, curly hair had popped out of the Bronco, and Caitlin ran to greet her.

"Emily!" Caitlin called.

"Caitlin!" Emily hugged her friend. "I'm so glad to see you."

A tall, handsome boy had also gotten out of the Bronco, and he and Jed were now standing together, watching the two girls.

"Honestly!" Jed shook his head. "You'd think they hadn't seen each other in years, instead of only last week."

Grinning, Matt nodded. "Girls!"

Raising his voice so Caitlin would be sure to hear, Jed said, "We'd never act that way."

Moving away from Emily, Caitlin turned and

put her hands on her hips. "You gentlemen are just jealous because nobody's hugging you," she observed.

Matt raised his eyebrows at Jed. "I think she's got a point," he said. They all laughed.

"I think we'd better get going," Caitlin suggested. "I know it's only fifty miles to Rock Ridge, but Mrs. Van Allen told me the last ten miles are over some pretty rough roads. I don't want to be late on our first day."

"Me either," Emily agreed. She climbed into the backseat, where she and Matt would be riding.

"Oh, I nearly forgot," Caitlin said when she saw Rollins, a portly, middle-aged man who served as both chauffeur and butler, start down the front steps carrying a large wicker hamper. "I had Mrs. Crowley pack a lunch for us. I thought it would be better to bring our lunch for the first few days—until we get to know our way around." Rollins packed the hamper into the back of the Bronco along with their other gear. Caitlin thanked him, then climbed into the front seat beside Jed.

Jed started the engine and put the Bronco in gear. As he drove down the tree-lined drive, Jed tapped his fingers lightly on the steering wheel and hummed a light tune. There was an air of enthusiasm in the car.

A half hour later, just after they had turned off the main highway, Emily sighed and said, "This country is so beautiful. I mean, just look over there." She gestured to a spot where wild blue flowers dotted the grass below some dogwood trees. Some white blossoms still clung to the trees' lower branches. "They look like hundreds of butterflies waiting to fly away."

"It *is* pretty, isn't it?" Caitlin answered in a soft voice. "I barely remember what this area looks like. I haven't been here since I was about seven, and that time it was in the winter. I was sitting in the backseat and couldn't see much, anyway."

"But you do remember some things about Rock Ridge, don't you?" Emily questioned. "Something that will help us today?"

"Not really. I remember that it was freezing. There were patches of snow on the ground and the people were all bundled up."

"Why did you go there?"

"I went with my grandmother, to hand out Christmas presents to the miners' children. I never went again. All I can remember are the green and red presents. . . ." Her words drifted off. Caitlin shook her head. "You know how it is with memories from when you were little."

"I know." Emily nodded. "Sometimes you only remember little bits, like the small pieces of a puzzle."

"I do remember one thing, though," Caitlin went on. "I remember seeing this one family who lived in an old abandoned bus. I couldn't get over that. I kept wondering how they could put any furniture inside—you know, with all the seats. I guess it never occurred to me that they would have removed the seats."

"How awful," Emily said in a sad voice.

"It really is," Matt said quietly.

"Hey, look!" Jed said in a hushed tone as he suddenly slowed the Bronco and brought it to a halt. "Look over there." He pointed toward the field to their right.

"What?" Emily whispered, peering around Matt. "Oh!" she said as she saw what he meant.

"Isn't he gorgeous?" Caitlin asked softly.

In silence they all watched as a white-tailed deer, who had been drinking from a stream beside the road, looked up at them. He didn't seem frightened. Instead, he gave them an almost haughty look, as if they had been rude to interrupt him. Moments later the deer bounded up the small bank and gracefully leaped through some laurels.

"You know," Emily said, "maybe it wouldn't be so bad living out here after all—I mean, being able to live in a place this beautiful."

"You mean," Jed added, "as long as you didn't have to live in an abandoned bus."

"Yeah, right," Emily said soberly. "I almost forgot about that. I guess it just seems impossible that people live like that in such a pretty place."

As Jed put the Bronco in gear, they started forward again, and Caitlin became lost in thought. She was still trying to remember more of her visit to Rock Ridge many years earlier. But she was only able to recall brief scenes, like so many still photographs. And her memories were in black and white. *No*, Caitlin thought, *that's wrong*. They were in tones of gray. The buildings had been gray, the wooden sidewalks had been gray, even the mud had been gray. But the children's faces had been different—rosy cheeked and full of excitement, except for one boy who had dark, dark gray eyes. They were hard and cold—frozen. She shook her head. Where had that memory come from? she wondered. She put the memory aside. It disturbed her, and Caitlin didn't want to enter Rock Ridge feeling any more nervous than she already did.

She turned her head and looked out the window at the West Virginia mountains. She would concentrate on that. Suddenly she noticed a small sign as they passed it: ROCK RIDGE: 1 MILE.

A moment later the Bronco rounded a bend. As it did, the lovely landscape abruptly ended. Jed involuntarily braked at the sight that lay before them—a raw, scarred hillside. The grass and trees had just disappeared.

"Oh, how horrible!" Matt blurted out. "Did Ryan Mining do all this?"

"Yes, it did," Caitlin replied in a low, angry voice.

"But why is it so bad?" Matt asked. "Why has so much of the landscape been destroyed?"

"It's from attempted strip mining," Caitlin answered. "Remember last fall, when we had our senior picnic on Ryan land? They had tried strip mining there, too, and the soil was stripped

33

away, also. We're letting the vegetation grow back there. And here the mining wasn't really successful."

"God, I'd hate to see what this place would look like if it had been successful," Matt said in a sarcastic tone.

"Okay, Matt," Jed said. "I think that's enough. You're acting as though it's Caitlin's fault. You know it's not."

"I'm sorry, Caitlin. I didn't mean to make you angry. But it is Ryan Mining's—"

"Matt!" This time it was Emily who spoke up."

"Hey, I'm sorry. Really." Matt shrugged. "It's just that this is so bad." He leaned back against the seat and was silent.

Jed put his foot on the gas again, and they drove down into the town, which lay at the bottom of the valley below them. Caitlin could see how the streets followed the natural line of the valley. The main street curved around the low hills.

As they moved slowly into town, Caitlin realized why the buildings of her memory were gray. They were built of unpainted boards that had become weathered. The sidewalks were the same. The hard-packed dirt street had a layer of coal dust mixed with the shale of the mine tailings or residue that gave it a darker gray color.

At the far end of the street stood a large, gray metal building. Caitlin knew what it was. It was the preparation plant, where the coal was washed and sorted as it came from the mine before being loaded into the trucks that would haul it away. Just above the plant was the black, gaping hole of the main entrance to the mine.

There were not many people on the street, only a few women with some children, and a couple of old men sitting in the sun in front of the general store.

"Caitlin," Jed spoke up, breaking the silence. No one had spoken since they had started down into the valley. "Do you have any idea where we're going? I don't see any numbers on any of the buildings."

"Yes," Caitlin answered in a voice that was quieter than normal. "I think it must be that place up there—where those two women are standing."

5

"Now, remember," Caitlin said as they pulled up to the two women who appeared to be waiting for them. "I'm using the name Westlake at first."

"Right," Emily said. "I won't forget." Jed and Matt nodded.

"I feel kind of nervous," Emily said.

"I know. Me, too."

"Well, break a leg, as those show biz folks say," Matt said.

Caitlin pushed down on the handle and opened the door. She paused to look back at Emily and Matt. "They look more nervous than we do. I think we're all a little scared of how this is going to turn out. Just try to look confident. And smile."

Following her own advice, she stepped down from the Bronco and walked over to the two women. "Hello!" She gave them a friendly smile. "Are you here to meet the people from Highgate Academy?"

"That's right!" The taller of the two women stepped forward. Obviously the spokeswoman, she tentatively held out a hand for Caitlin to shake. "And would you be Miss Westlake?"

"Yes," she replied, taking the woman's hand and giving it a friendly shake. "And these are my friends." She turned to introduce them. "This is Emily Michaels, Matt Jenks, and Jed Michaels."

"This is Jenny Sumney," the woman said, looking at her friend. "And I'm Lola Butler."

Caitlin hesitated for a moment before saying, "Lola Butler. Why, yes, of course." For a second Caitlin was confused. She had talked to a Lola Butler on the phone. But Caitlin had assumed from the things the woman had said that she was not older than thirty. Yet the woman standing in front of her seemed middle-aged. She looked closer to forty than to thirty. Well, Caitlin told herself, being a miner's wife had to be hard. "Of course I remember," she went on. Caitlin didn't want the woman to guess the real reason she had hesitated. "It's only that it's been a few weeks since then, and—"

"And you've been busy with graduating from high school. Well, I'm sure I can guess what an exciting time that must have been," Lola Butler said graciously.

"Yes, that's true." Caitlin smiled her agreement. "Is this the building we're to use?" She turned to gesture toward the building in front of them.

"Right, ma'am," Jenny Sumney said. She stepped toward the door. "We got it all nice and

clean for you. You want to take a look at it now?"
She put her hand on the doorknob.

"Oh, yes. Please." Caitlin stepped over to the
door. "Tell me, how long do we have before the
children arrive? I need to know how much time
we have to get set up."

"Oh, you got a good ten minutes." Mrs. Butler
smiled. "At least that much."

"Ten minutes!" Caitlin closed her eyes to try to
contain her exasperation. She had hoped they'd
have at least an hour. She wanted time to get
everything exactly the way they wanted it, to
put away the supplies they'd brought, find
electrical outlets, test the audio and video equipment, maybe even set up a makeshift stage
where the children could perform little skits. *Oh,
well*, she thought. They would simply have to do
the best they could with the time they had. And
it was up to her to get the show on the road.
Opening her eyes, she managed a pleased look.
"All right. We'll be ready."

Turning to Matt and Jed, she said, "Would you
please get the equipment from the Bronco, while
Emily and I go inside?"

"Sure," Matt said, giving her a mock salute
and turning smartly around. Then he and Jed
started toward the Bronco.

Caitlin and Emily followed the two women
into the building. Once inside, Caitlin looked
around in disbelief. The room was completely
bare, except for a small wooden table in one
corner. "There's no furniture—nothing to sit on,

or draw on, or play games on." She turned to Mrs. Butler. "The room is empty."

Lola Butler looked embarrassed. "Well," she explained, "there wasn't all that much to spare, Miss Westlake. We thought you could use that table over there for your supplies. And the young'uns'll do just fine sitting on the floor. But I guess we just didn't think. Tell you what. I can go to my house and get some chairs for you and the others."

"Oh, no, thank you." Caitlin laid a hand gently on the woman's arm. "It's really all right. We'll do just fine with what we've got. Please don't go to any trouble."

"Are you sure?"

"Yes. Absolutely," Caitlin said in a firm voice.

"Well, then, okay," Mrs. Butler agreed. Caitlin was sure that the woman would have brought her only chairs if Caitlin had asked. "We'll go tell the children you're here," Lola said.

As the woman left, Caitlin let out a heavy sigh. Glancing around her, she tried to decide what to do first. As Jed and Matt came in with the supplies a few minutes later, she had her battle plan ready.

A couple of hours later she stood at the back of the room, watching as Emily and Matt led the children through a song. The children on Matt's side of the room sang the words about different animals, while Emily's half of the room had to answer them with the appropriate animal sounds. They seemed to be having a great time, even sitting cross-legged on the hard wooden floor.

Walking over to Jed, she said in a quiet voice, "I'd like to take a short break, to get my second wind. Would you mind if I left for about ten or fifteen minutes?"

"Go ahead." Jed looked up from loading a cartoon cassette into the VCR they had brought along. "If anyone deserves a break right now, you do. You really got this whole thing off the ground. And under pretty adverse conditions, too."

"Thanks." She squeezed his arm affectionately, wishing she could kiss him instead. "I'll be back in plenty of time to hand out the art supplies when you've finished with the cartoon."

"Okay." He smiled at her tenderly.

She went out the door and began walking along the wooden sidewalk. Caitlin thought that the town looked very much like the ones in old western movies. It had the same wooden walks, and there was even benches on either side of the door of the general store. The benches were vacant now, and she decided to sit down for a while. The sun warmed her, and she closed her eyes, leaning back against the splintery side of the building.

Caitlin began to feel drowsy in the warm June sunshine. She thought back to her first and last visit to Rock Ridge, trying to remember more details. It had been just before Christmas, and it was very cold outside, that she could recall. She had come with her grandmother to help hand out gifts of toys and clothing to the children. It was an annual affair, but that was the first time Caitlin had been considered old enough to come along, and she had been excited about playing Santa Claus. It had made her feel quite grown-up.

Now the whole memory came flooding back, perfectly preserved. As she stepped out of the heated limousine onto the frozen mud of the street, the bitter temperature had been a shock. But Caitlin stood tall, as her grandmother expected her to, in her fur-trimmed hat and coat, while Rollins brought the boxes of brightly wrapped presents to her from the trunk of the Bentley. Her grandmother had already explained that the boxes wrapped in green were for the boys and the red ones were for the girls. She warned Caitlin several times not to get them mixed up.

Rollins had stood beside her holding the packages, and she reached for a green box first. She wanted the first gift to go to a boy. But three of the small children couldn't wait for her to hand the presents out one at a time. They had begun to crowd around her, reaching out for the presents. Then one of the older children had reached toward her as well. Vividly she recalled how his ragged sweater, torn jeans, and dirty fingers had repelled her. She had screamed with surprise and fright, backing up against Rollins's legs as she tried to get away from the boy.

Rollins had dropped the stack of presents, and they tumbled in a heap at his feet.

Mrs. Ryan had taken charge quickly. But instead of comforting Caitlin, Mrs. Ryan had shoved her firmly into the back of the limousine. She told Caitlin to stay there and not move. Then she had handed out the presents while Caitlin watched.

Caitlin watched the ragged boy step back and pull away from the other children. But he continued to stare at her through the window of the limousine. He had stayed there until the gift giving was over and her grandmother returned to the car. Finally Rollins had hopped into the driver's seat, and the boy watched as they drove away. Caitlin vividly remembered those eyes. They had been cold and gray and full of hate.

As Caitlin slowly opened her eyes, she shuddered in the warm sun.

The sun was already low in the western sky when Jed drove the Bronco through the stone pillars at the entrance to Ryan Acres. But instead of driving straight up to the mansion, he stopped halfway up the drive, beside one of the white-painted pasture fences.

They had dropped Emily and Matt off in town for hamburgers. Jed planned to join them and drive Emily home after he had a few minutes alone with Caitlin.

"Whew!" Jed let out a long sigh as he switched

off the engine. "This has definitely been one of the longest days of my life."

"I know," Caitlin said in a tired voice.

"But it was worthwhile, don't you think?"

"Absolutely."

Turning slightly in his seat, he put a hand on Caitlin's arm. "Do you mind if we stop here for a second? I have this vision of Rollins waiting by the door, ready to rush down the stairs and help you out of the car. I just wanted to be alone for a minute."

"I know what you mean," Caitlin said, smiling.

He stroked her arm lightly. "Anyway, now I can say goodbye to you without Rollins peering over our shoulders."

Caitlin smiled again. She was exhausted and was looking forward to dinner, a hot bath, and a chance to relax.

"I also want to tell you how proud I am of you," Jed said in a low voice. "You were great today. And those kids loved you."

"Do you really think so?"

"Uh-huh. Especially that one little girl who sat in the front row. She never took her eyes off you."

"Oh, Kathy Stokes. Yeah, she's a real cutie. And she's so smart. I swear, if I hadn't stopped her, she would have answered every question I asked them." Caitlin placed her fingers lightly on Jed's cheek, softly running them down along his jaw. "But how about you? You were pretty terrific yourself, you know that."

"Was I really?" The corners of his mouth turned up in a teasing little smile. "Well, yes. I guess I was."

"Jed Michaels! I don't believe you!" Pulling her hand away from him, she made a fist and gave him a playful punch. She opened her hand slowly and ran it over the firm muscles beneath Jed's thin cotton shirt. In a low, soft voice, Caitlin said, "Well, you were terrific. You really were." She let out a small sigh and slipped her hand around his neck. "Jed, I love you so very much. You're everything I need. Everything I'll ever want. I couldn't stand it if we were ever separated again—like last summer."

"Oh, Caitlin, my beautiful Caitlin." Jed shifted in the seat so he could put his arms around her and pull her close. "Can't we just forget about last summer?" he murmured. "Can't we just think about the future?" He kissed her tenderly on the forehead. "Because, I promise, we're going to have the best future any two people ever had." He kissed her again, this time on the cheek. "We'll never let anything come between us again. You'll see—never."

He ran his hands up over her shoulders and placed them on either side of her face. Looking deep into her blue eyes, he went on, "And that's a promise I am going to keep." He touched his lips to hers, gently at first. Then his kisses became firmer, filled with emotion, as Jed realized once again how much he loved Caitlin.

6

Toward the end of her first week at Rock Ridge, Caitlin got into a conversation with two miners' wives. She had been taking a break and was sitting outside the general store, going over some new project ideas she had for the program. Two women were sitting on the other bench. Gradually parts of the women's conversation began to filter in through her thoughts, and Caitlin realized they were talking about some problems at the mine. Trying not to look too obvious, she began to listen.

"The way I heard it is," one was saying, "the main entrance fan went down. It almost caused an explosion, 'cause the mine hadn't been dusted for so long."

"Ain't that just the way!"

Caitlin raised her head and glanced over at them. The first woman shook her head, then added, "What I can't figure is how come those mine people can't do what the government regulations say they're supposed to do."

"You're right, Andeline," the other woman

45

agreed. "Still, maybe it's better to die quick instead of coughing yourself to death with black lung like that Ray Stokes is doing. Poor Peggy— and with little Kathy and those two older boys to raise."

"Well, if they'd only spray like they're supposed to, wouldn't neither one happen."

Caitlin couldn't sit there quietly any longer. She had to find out more. If Ryan Mining was operating unsafe mines, Caitlin wanted to know about it.

"Excuse me," she said as she walked over to where the women were sitting. "I couldn't help but overhear your conversation. Would you mind telling me what rock dusting is—and why not doing it could cause an explosion?"

At first they looked up at her as if she were butting in where she didn't belong. But then Andeline softened. Patting the empty spot beside her, she said, "If you really want to know, come sit down and we'll tell you."

Caitlin sat beside Andeline and listened while the women told her about the mine's safety problems. They used many local words and expressions that Caitlin had never heard before, but she got the gist of what they were saying.

The women told Caitlin that one of the biggest hazards facing miners was the threat of explosions in the mines. The combination of coal dust and methane gas, which was present in coal formations, was very flammable. It could be touched off, they told her, by a slight spark from any piece of heavy machinery used in the mine.

To prevent these explosions, the mine operators made sure the newly exposed coal was "dusted"—sprayed with powdered limestone—regularly, keeping the coal dust from mixing with the methane. Spraying the coal with water also helped. So, it didn't seem to be a matter of cost so much as making sure these procedures were done regularly.

Large fans were also placed at the mine entrances and exits to help blow away the excess dust. But these fans broke down often, adding to the danger.

"And all of this is regulated by the government?" Caitlin asked when Andeline had stopped talking.

Andeline nodded emphatically. "Sure it is. But them regulations don't mean diddly. They're just vague enough to let the mine owner get away with murder. And I do mean murder."

"But that's horrible," Caitlin gasped, forgetting for a moment who she was. "Someone should do something about this."

"You're right, miss, someone should," the other woman spoke up. "I dare you to go tell that old Mrs. Ryan what you think." She paused to turn and point toward the end of the street, at the imposing entrance to the mine. "She owns that mine." She looked back at Caitlin. "But it won't do no good. The way I hear, she's real hardheaded—she don't listen to nobody." The woman narrowed her eyes. "Unless you're there to tell her how to make more money."

When the woman had switched from talking

47

about the mine's safety problems to telling her about the person she blamed for their troubles, Caitlin felt a knot grow in the pit of her stomach. They were accusing her grandmother of being thoughtless, greedy, and uncaring. But Caitlin knew they were wrong—terribly wrong. Her grandmother was very businesslike, but she cared about people. Perhaps she simply didn't know what was going on there. Maybe she just needed to be told, to be convinced that she should find out about the problems in Rock Ridge. Caitlin promised herself that she was going to talk to her grandmother about the mines. And Caitlin vowed she would make sure her grandmother listened.

But when she told Jed about her plans later that day, he told her to wait. "Listen, I know you'd love to go talk to her as soon as you get home tonight. But think this out thoroughly first. Remember how your grandmother thinks—she doesn't listen to anyone but experts."

"Yes. So?"

"Okay." He nodded. "And remember how tough your grandmother can be. I mean, all you've got right now is some idle village gossip."

"But, Jed, I can't just do nothing. That fan problem really sounds serious."

"I know. I know." Jed took her hand. "But just listen to me for a minute. Since we're obviously not experts, there's no reason why she should listen to what either of us has to say. But what if we could present her with some concrete facts, some statistics, when we go to talk to her?"

"Did you say *we*?"

"Of course." Jed grinned. "Did you think I'd make you deal with this alone?"

"Well—" she hesitated. "But it's my problem."

"Not really," he reasoned. "It's the problem of everyone in this town. And I've grown to like them all. Especially the kids. And if what you heard is true, that little Kathy Stokes's father has black lung disease, then that sort of brings it home even harder. We've got to help them if we can."

"You know I met Kathy's mother yesterday. They live way out at the edge of town. One of the other mothers usually brings Kathy in with her children, but Mrs. Stokes did get to come yesterday. Now I understand why she doesn't get into town very much. She probably has to stay at home to take care of her husband."

"Yeah," Jed said thoughtfully. "I can't even begin to imagine how terrible it must be to watch someone you love die from a disease he got from working to support his family. It seems so unfair."

"Well, that's why we've got to do something."

"Look, I'll take the morning off and go to the library and the government offices tomorrow and get all the information I can on mining safety. You keep talking to the women around here on your breaks. They obviously like you. Then, *after* we have all the facts, we'll talk to your grandmother."

49

Caitlin nodded in agreement. "I think it sounds perfect."

"The thing is, it isn't your grandmother's responsibility to stay on top of all of the regulations and the day-to-day details. There must be a professional engineer, or manager, or someone who oversees the general running of Ryan Mining. That means we'll be telling your grandmother that someone on her staff isn't doing his or her job. No one likes to hear something like that. We'll have to be very diplomatic about the whole thing."

"Umm." Caitlin's expression was glum. "I think we've got another problem. Grandmother is not the kind of person who can easily admit that she's wrong."

"But she's fair, Caitlin. And when it's important, she'll do what she knows is right, no matter how hard it is for her. She did when it came to telling you about your father, didn't she?" he reminded her gently.

"You're right, Jed." Caitlin smiled. "And this is important, too. Grandmother will have to listen. She just will!"

"Yes, I think she will." Jed put his arm around Caitlin's shoulders. "You can be very convincing when you want to be. I remember how you practically ran Highgate when you were president of the student council. You had everyone on their toes."

Caitlin looked up at him mischievously. "Not you, Jed Michaels. If I remember right, it took me awhile to convince you that I was the right girl for you."

"Ah, but you finally did." Jed turned so he could nuzzle the side of her neck. "And I'm very glad."

She turned and looked directly at him. "Glad enough to come to a party at Ryan Acres Saturday night?"

"Oh, no!" Jed groaned. "You mean one of your grandmother's business parties, don't you?" Caitlin nodded. "Do I really have to?"

"Yes, you do. I won't take no for an answer," she insisted.

"Are you sure?" He gave her a lopsided grin.

"I'm positive." She changed her tactics. "Please come, Jed," she begged. "Grandmother's guests are always so much older than I am. I need to have someone there my own age— a little moral support."

Jed sighed. "Oh, all right. But I'm only giving in because I love you so much."

"And I love you for making the sacrifice," she countered.

"Ooh." Jed leaned closer. "How about backing that statement up with a kiss?"

"I'd be happy to," Caitlin said, putting her arms around him.

7

Caitlin opened the velvet jeweler's box and lifted out an exquisite necklace of emeralds and diamonds. Leaning toward the mirror, she fastened it around her neck, then lightly ran her fingers along the intricate design of sparkling gems. Three large emeralds formed the centers a diamond starbursts, linked together by a delicate platinum chain. Each perfectly faceted gem reflected back prisms of light from the overhead chandelier. It was truly beautiful. She had been given the necklace only the week before. It was a graduation present from her grandmother, designed especially for Caitlin by a famous New York jeweler.

Caitlin smiled at her reflection, knowing that both her father and Jed would be coming to the party that night and knowing she would look her best for them.

Caitlin stepped back from the full-length mirror and turned to admire the total effect of her hair, the necklace, and her new dress. She had piled her hair high on her head in curls to match the style of the dress. The dress was made of the finest white voile, with tiny purple forget-me-nots embroidered on it. It had a wide, ruffled, off-the-shoulder neckline and a fitted waist. The full skirt came to just above her ankles. On her feet were slender-strapped, high-heeled sandals the same color as the tiny purple flowers.

She was pleased with her reflection, recalling that the woman at the dress shop had said she looked like a modern-day Scarlet O'Hara. Caitlin spun around so that the skirt belled out. She wished she had one of those delicate parasols southern ladies used to carry. That would really have completed the picture.

Her father was not bringing a date to the party, and since Jed had said he would be late, she would have some time alone with her father. She hoped he had already arrived. The sounds of people arriving had been drifting up from downstairs for nearly half an hour.

With one final look in the mirror and a touch to her already perfect hair, she turned and went to the door. She walked down the long hallway to the top of the stairs, paused, took a breath, then gracefully descended the curving staircase.

The high-ceilinged living room was crowded with laughing and chatting guests, who were drinking champagne from fluted glasses and nibbling hors d'oeuvres that were passed by waitresses who had been hired for the evening from a catering service. The highly polished antique furniture glowed in the light of the crystal chandeliers, while the ice green and peach brocades of the sofas and chairs formed a perfect setting for the people who preferred to sit as they talked.

At the far end of the room, a string quartet played Vivaldi. The french doors on either side of them opened onto the terrace and allowed the warm night air to circulate through the room. It was through one of those open doors that Caitlin thought she saw her father. At least, the tall handsome man with dark hair looked very much like her father. It was difficult for her to really tell because she had to look past and around the people standing in between them. He was looking out at the lawn and holding a glass of champagne. She started forward, anxious to talk to him.

She had only gone a few feet, however, when a slim hand, wearing a large sapphire ring, touched her arm. With only the slightest pressure, her grandmother stopped her.

"Caitlin," Mrs. Ryan said, her voice low, "please don't rush through the room like that. People will think you are extremely rude if you dash by them that way." She paused to smile and nod at someone behind Caitlin's shoulder. "You passed right by Mr. and Mrs. Turner without so much as a word."

"I'm sorry," Caitlin apologized. "But I thought I saw my father out on the terrace. I wanted to speak with him."

"Well, you can do that later. There are a number of very influential people here tonight, and you must be a polite hostess. Do remember this is a business party. It may not seem to be, but it is." She paused again, this time to call a greeting to Mr. and Mrs. Jankowitz from Ryan Mining's Washington office. Looking back at Caitlin, Mrs. Ryan said, "You will remember that, won't you, dear?" Her grandmother patted her arm. Then, as Caitlin nodded, Mrs. Ryan noticed someone else and left her granddaughter. Moving toward a white-haired gentleman, she said, "Good evening, Senator. How nice of you to come. Have you tried the smoked pheasant—our own birds. . . ."

Free once more, Caitlin wanted to head straight for the terrace. But she knew she must do as her grandmother had requested and mingle first.

Seeing a middle-aged couple she knew from the Virginia hunt season, she strolled over to them. "Hello, Mr. and Mrs. Vanderplum. How are you?"

"Why, hello, Caitlin," Mrs. Vanderplum said. "It's so nice to see you again. It's been some months—last fall, I think?"

"Yes," Caitlin replied. "At the Appleveil hunt."

"Oh, yes!" Mr. Vanderplum spoke up. "If I recall, you rode magnificently—and quite daringly."

"Thank you," Caitlin said graciously. Then she added in a modest voice, "But I really have to give most of the credit to my horse, Duster. Now that he's no longer a green hunter, I think he's one of the finest I've ever seen."

"Ah, and you're not alone." Mr. Vanderplum's eyes twinkled. "One of the Crawford boys told me that he couldn't decide which was more beautiful—the horse or the rider."

"Well, thank you again."

"Charles"—Mrs. Vanderplum put her hand on her husband's arm—"I do believe you're embarrassing the girl."

"Why?" He winked at Caitlin. "I'm only reporting the truth."

Caitlin laughed lightly. "And I love hearing it," she said. "But now, if you'll excuse me, I see some other people I must say hello to."

With a smile, she moved away, angling in the direction of the terrace door. Spotting two older women, friends of her grandmother's as well as the wives of Ryan Mining executives, she went up to them. "Good evening, Mrs. Emerich. Mrs. O'Keefe."

"Why good evening, Caitlin," they both said at nearly the same time.

"How lovely to see you," Mrs. Emerich added. "And I understand congratulations are in order. You've graduated from Highgate, I hear. And your grandmother tells me you were the class valedictorian."

"Well, I gave the valedictorian speech," Caitlin replied. "But it was only because the girl who should have had the honor came down with the flu the day before graduation. I was second in my class."

"Still," Mrs. O'Keefe interjected, "being second is impressive, especially considering High-gate's excellent reputation."

"My grandmother has always insisted that I keep up my grades," Caitlin demurred.

"You've given her good reason to be proud of you."

"I only hope I'll do as well in college—" Caitlin pretended to see someone motioning to her. "Oh, I hope you will excuse me. There's someone over there who wants to speak with me."

Caitlin had almost reached the door to the terrace. She had only to stop for one more brief moment as another friend of her grandmother's complimented her on her dress and asked where she had gotten it.

When she finally did reach the terrace, it was empty except for two middle-aged men who were smoking cigars and laughing over something one had told the other.

Turning, she looked across the room, searching for her father's familiar dark head. But, with all the men dressed in white dinner jackets, it was nearly impossible to tell one from the other.

Suddenly Caitlin thought she had spotted him, and she was starting toward him when she heard her name being called from nearby. The voice was all too familiar. It belonged to the guest of honor for the evening—Colin Wollman. Even before she turned to reply, she could feel her stomach churning. Taking a deep breath, she turned around and smiled.

"Hello, Mr. Wollman," she said politely. "How nice to see you. How are you?"

"Very well, Caitlin. Very well." He smiled at her. The smile was warm, but Caitlin knew it was just for show. It made her want to scowl back. "It's a lovely party. I've already thanked Regina. It was so thoughtful of her to give it so that I would have a chance to meet more of her friends."

"I'm so glad you're enjoying it." Caitlin answered automatically. She was noticing the pretty blond woman standing beside Mr. Wollman, wondering who she was. Was he serious about her, or was she just a friend? Caitlin knew, from what her grandmother had said, that Mr. Wollman wasn't married.

"Pardon me for not introducing you immediately," he said, noticing her interest. "This is my sister, Nicole. Nicole Wollman, I'd like you to meet Caitlin Ryan."

"How do you do, Caitlin?" Nicole's voice was low, almost sultry. They didn't look at all alike, Caitlin thought. Perhaps they weren't full brother and sister.

"It's very nice to meet you," Caitlin said. "Are you visiting?"

"Yes—and no." She put a slim hand on Colin Wollman's arm. Her long, pink nails shimmered against the white silk of his jacket. "I'm visiting right now. But since Colin's going to be the new attorney at Ryan Mining, he's asked me if I would like to move down here to Virginia to be closer to him." She smiled. Her amber eyes slanted up slightly at the corners as she did, giving her a vaguely exotic look. "Our parents died some time ago, so we're the only family we have."

"I'm sorry," Caitlin said. "But I'm sure you'll like Virginia—and being so near your brother." Caitlin suddenly couldn't find anything to say. She realized that she didn't like Nicole Wollman any more than she liked her brother. But she couldn't pinpoint the reason, and that bothered her.

"Living here should be fun," Nicole continued after an awkward pause. "Colin has offered to buy into a small designer boutique for me, so I'll be a part owner."

"How interesting," Caitlin responded, wondering how Colin could afford to be so generous when he was just starting as her grandmother's attorney. But then, she didn't know much about him or his background. Perhaps he had made a lot of money before or had family money. "Have you done that sort of thing before?" she asked Nicole.

"Well—" Nicole began.

"The shop is in Alexandria," Colin said. "You'll have to drive up there and see it after Nicole has made the changes she has in mind."

"Yes," Nicole said. "I'm planning on stocking more clothes that will appeal to the college set." She looked at Caitlin's dress. "That, by the way, is a lovely gown. Did you buy it in town?"

"No, I got it in Georgetown," Caitlin answered. *That's weird*, she thought. Her dress had been made by Georgette Paxton, a very popular clothing designer for young women. Nicole should have recognized her work. *Well*, Caitlin thought, *maybe she knows more about casual clothing. But still—*

"Hi, Caitlin." Jed's voice, coming from behind her, startled her; she had not seen him come in.

"Jed, hello!" Caitlin swung around, very glad to see him. Now she would have an excuse to leave these people. But first she had to be polite and make introductions.

"Jed, this is Colin Wollman and his sister, Nicole Wollman. Mr. Wollman is my grandmother's new attorney." She put her hand lightly on Jed's arm. "This is Jed Michaels. We went to Highgate together."

"Hello, Jed," Mr. Wollman said pleasantly. He put out his hand for Jed to shake.

"Nice to meet you, Mr. Wollman." Jed shook his hand. He turned to Nicole. "And you, too, Miss Wollman."

"Nicole, please." She smiled at Jed with obvious interest.

Caitlin felt a sudden stab of—what? Jealousy? But that was ridiculous, she told herself. Nicole had to be in her mid-thirties. She was much too old for Jed. But there was no mistaking the look in her eyes. And to Caitlin's horror, Jed was returning her charming smile.

"Jed—" To get his attention, she put her hand on his arm again. "I was just about to go look for my father. Would you like to come with me?" She squeezed his arm to let him know that she wanted to leave.

"Of course."

"Will you excuse us?" Caitlin took a step backward, pulling Jed's arm.

"Certainly," Colin Wollman replied. "We'll probably have another chance to talk before the evening is over."

"Yes. I hope so." Caitlin nodded and smiled politely. But as soon as she and Jed were far enough away that they wouldn't hear, she muttered, "Not if I can help it!"

"Caitlin!" Jed glanced down at her. "What's the matter with you? Did something happen before I came?"

Caitlin sighed and shook her head. "No. We were all very polite."

"Well, then. Why the big rush to get away? I mean, I just met them— Oh, is that the attorney who gives you the creeps? Is he the one your grandmother chose?"

"Uh-huh. Tell me, what did you think of Nicole Wollman?"

"What do you mean, what did I think of her? You dragged me away as soon as I'd said hello."

"Did you think she was pretty?"

"Sure!" Suddenly Jed understood what she was getting at. He grinned and said, "For an older woman, that is."

Relieved, Caitlin answered his smile by tucking her arm through his and squeezing it. This time it was a happy squeeze. She was with one of the two men she loved most in the world. All she had to do was find the other, and her evening would be complete.

Caitlin and Jed wandered out to the terrace,

where there were some guests who wanted to speak with Caitlin. When she and Jed returned to the living room, Caitlin was shocked to see that her father was standing, talking to Nicole Wollman. She saw her father move even closer to Nicole, as if whispering some secret meant only for her ears.

Don't let that woman fool you! Caitlin screamed silently. *She's no good, believe me!*

Gordon Westlake obviously didn't agree with his daughter, for he smiled warmly at Nicole. He appeared totally captivated by the beautiful blond.

Caitlin turned to Jed. "We've got to get that horrible woman away from my father."

"Caitlin," Jed protested in a low voice, "I don't know why you're so upset. You barely know Nicole Wollman."

"Jed, I can't tell you why I know she's no good, but I do. Trust me on this, please."

Jed turned to face Caitlin and put his hands firmly on her shoulders. "No, I won't. And what's more, I won't let you ruin your father's evening. If Nicole is as terrible as you think she is, he'll find out soon enough. Now, let's just try to enjoy the party."

Reluctantly, Caitlin agreed. Giving her father and Nicole one last glance, she promised herself that, whatever it took, she would discover the secrets of Nicole Wollman.

8

When Caitlin came out the front door on Monday morning, she was surprised to see only Jed and Emily waiting for her in the Bronco.

"Where's Matt?" she asked, concerned.

"Jed, let me tell her." Emily leaned out the window. "Caitlin, remember how Matt wished us luck the first day we went to Rock Ridge by saying, 'Break a leg!'?"

Caitlin stared at Emily for a second while the news sunk in. "Oh, no! Are you serious? I don't believe it—Matt broke his leg? When? How? Why didn't you tell me about it sooner?"

"One question at a time," Jed said. "Climb in, and I'll tell you what happened on the way."

As soon as Emily had climbed into the back and Caitlin had buckled herself into the front seat, Jed put the Bronco in gear and pulled away.

"So, explain," Caitlin demanded as she turned toward Jed.

"It's not all that interesting," Jed said. "Except, I guess, to Matt. He broke his leg playing soccer."

"Oh, great! When did he do this?"

"Yesterday."

"And you didn't call and tell me! Matt is an important part of what we do. Now we'll have to figure out how to divide the work among three people instead of four," she said, exasperated. "Jed, honestly, you should have called me."

"Caitlin, come on." Jed tried to calm her down. "Sure, it's going to be tough without Matt, but we can do it. And, really, what would you have done yesterday? Nothing. I figured you didn't need to sit around and be upset for a whole day. Okay?" They had come to a corner, and Jed stopped to let another car cross the intersection. He looked over at her. "Angry?"

She looked back at him. He had such a cute, worried little-boy look on his face that she couldn't help smiling. "No, I guess not. And I suppose you did do the right thing. I couldn't have done anything yesterday—except worry, as you said." Suddenly a thought occurred to her. "What about flowers? Is Matt at home?"

"Yes." Jed stepped on the gas again. "It wasn't a bad break, so they just set it and let him go. And he said to tell you not to send flowers— guess he knows you pretty well." Jed laughed. "But he said he could definitely use some books or magazines."

"He's got them," Caitlin said. "I'll have Rollins deliver some tomorrow." She sank back against the seat and closed her eyes, going over in her mind the activities she had planned for the week. She had to reassign the things Matt would have done. A few minutes later, she opened her eyes and turned to Jed. "Instead of helping the older kids make those papier-mâché puppets of early miners, could you help the younger boys finish off the fort? Emily"—she turned around to look at her friend—"maybe you could do the puppets while I help the younger girls make Scots' tams. You're so much more artistic than I am."

As Caitlin worked with the children, she found she liked some of them better than others, although she tried hard not to let it show. One of her favorites was little Kathy Stokes. Because her father was sick and could no longer work in the mine, Kathy's family was poorer than the other mining families. She expected so little and was always so thrilled when anyone was kind to her.

"She's such a funny combination of adult and child," Caitlin told Jed on Thursday after they dropped Emily off. "One minute she'll be telling me all about the fairies she swears live in the woods behind her house, and the next minute she'll be telling me about all the work she does at home to help. Jed, she's just a little girl!" Caitlin was silent for a moment. "It makes me want to do extravagant things like bring her home with me and buy her hundreds of pretty dresses and take her riding on a merry-go-round. Is that silly, Jed?"

"No, of course it's not silly," Jed replied. But it

was as if he weren't really listening to her. He sounded almost distant.

"Jed?"

"Um-hmm."

"You're not really listening to me, are you?"

"Yes, I am. Well, no—I guess I'm not," he admitted. "I'm sorry. It's just that I've been thinking—about talking to your grandmother. Maybe it's not such a hot idea after all."

"What are you talking about?"

"Caitlin, I think those women you first talked to about the problems in the mine might have been exaggerating a little."

"What? What are you talking about?" She stared at Jed. "They sounded like they were telling the truth to me."

"Well, sure," Jed replied. "Coal mining isn't the least dangerous profession in the world. Look, I've been doing some talking to people and snooping around myself. And, well, what I've heard is mostly just gripes about having to work extra shifts and getting tired. They aren't as conscientious as they might be around the machines, but they're still not careless. And the fan *has* gone down a couple of times. But it's no one's fault. It's broken down, that's all. And things do break down, you know."

"Jed!" Caitlin stared at him. "Do you hear what you're saying? Extra-long shifts! A fan that keeps breaking down! You're talking about small things, yes, but things that can cause serious accidents. What if there were an explosion? Dozens of people would be killed. Jed, these are

exactly the things I want to tell my grandmother."

"But what I'm trying to tell you, Caitlin, is that
Ryan Mining isn't doing anything illegal. And,
to be perfectly honest, there haven't been any
major accidents in Rock Ridge for several years."

"Great. That's just great, Jed." Caitlin crossed
her arms and began drumming her fingers.
"You're always the one who wants to save the
whole world. Now you sound just like one of
those cops on TV who says, 'Sorry, ma'am, but
until the man who's threatening to kill you
actually does, we can't do anything about him.'"

"Caitlin, please," Jed said evenly. "Try to
understand."

"I am!" she insisted hotly. "You're the one
who doesn't understand."

"I don't?" Jed shot back.

"Not if you're going to dismiss the whole
thing like this."

They drove in silence for several minutes.
Finally Jed relented. "All right, all right. You can
stop with the cold-shoulder treatment. We can
talk to your grandmother just as we planned.
When do you want to do it?"

"Well, I wish we could talk to her this weekend, but that's impossible. She's going to be in
Washington until Monday. She's going to some
kind of ceremony at Ford's Theatre. But maybe
the next weekend? I don't want to do it in the
middle of the week because she'll have other
things on her mind. You could come over for the
day one weekend, and we could swim and ride

and just relax. Then after dinner, we can all go into the library and talk." Caitlin smiled happily at her plan.

Taking his eyes off the road long enough to smile at her wryly, Jed said, "You sound as if you're sitting in that big leather chair in the Ryan Mining presidential office already. Caitlin"—he suddenly sounded serious—"do you think you might do that? I mean, has working with the people out in Rock Ridge made you change your mind about someday taking over Ryan Mining?"

"Please, Jed!" Caitlin rolled her eyes. "Do I really look like the kind of person who'd do that?"

"Well, up until recently, I would have said no. But now I'm beginning to wonder."

"You can just stop wondering, okay? I'm just worried about getting some of those safety problems taken care of, that's all. All I really want to think about is going to Montana with you and learning how to rope a fence post."

"Rope a fence post?" Jed looked confused.

"What a short memory you have, Jed Michaels," Caitlin teased. "Don't you remember? When we first talked about my going out to visit your ranch, you promised to teach me how to rope. And you said the only thing that wouldn't run away was a fence post, so I should learn to rope one of them first."

"A short memory! I must have said that a year ago." He grinned. "Well, all right, then. I'm giving fair warning to all the fence posts in Montana. Look out! Caitlin's on her way!"

* * *

Caitlin was continuing to grow closer to little Kathy Stokes. And Kathy seemed to feel the same way about Caitlin. Every morning she would run through the door and charge up to Caitlin for a good-morning hug. And she wouldn't leave in the afternoon without her goodbye hug. And through Kathy's stories about her friends and her family, Caitlin learned a lot about the miners and their ways.

Kathy also liked to talk about her family. She was the youngest and the only girl. The person she loved most was her oldest brother. And she kept telling Caitlin she had to meet him. The Wednesday of the third week of the program she told Caitlin that she had asked her brother to come and pick her up, so Caitlin must wait until he came. Caitlin promised. The two of them were waiting in the empty room after the other children had left. Emily and Jed had gone to the general store to get some sodas.

"You'll really love him, Caitlin," Kathy said. "He's smart, just like you."

"Oh? Why is he so smart, Kathy?" Caitlin asked. She was touched by the little girl's adoration of her brother.

"Jake knows everything. He knows all about the stars, and about the different kinds of rocks that are in the ground, and about what makes animals sick and how to make them well. He made our dog well when he got sick last year, and everyone else said we should put him to sleep. And he knows other things, too, like all about herbs—just like the herb lady in town—"

"You're right, Kathy," Caitlin replied when the little girl ran out of breath. "He sounds really smart. I'll bet he's a big help to your mother."

Just at that moment the tall figure of Jake Stokes appeared in the doorway, though neither Caitlin nor Kathy saw him. Jake heard only the final words Caitlin had spoken. To him, they sounded pitying, rather than complimentary, as Caitlin had meant them to be.

With a long-festering hostility—from having been born the son of a poor coal miner—he was about to march into the room and tell that snotty rich girl exactly what he thought of her. But then Caitlin moved slightly, and the light streaming in from the doorway fell on her delicate features. Seeing her face for the first time, he froze. He knew that girl. He knew her and hated her—he had hated her for eleven years!

He tried to remember what Kathy had called her when she told him about her. She always referred to her as "the beautiful lady." But, he thought, she *had* also mentioned her name. He remembered—Westlake—her name was supposed to be Westlake. He smiled grimly. Well, he knew better. Obviously she had used a false name to fool the people of Rock Ridge. But he knew who she really was. *Caitlin Ryan*. He spat out the name in his mind. Oh, he knew her all right. He had been following her life in the society pages of newspapers ever since the

Christmas when he was ten. Now there she was—in person—not twelve feet from him. *Caitlin Ryan*, the rich little brat who had screamed at him when all he'd wanted to do was touch the beautiful coat she had been wearing. He hadn't meant to hurt her; he had only wanted to touch, just for a moment, someone who was so rich she could afford to wear a coat like that. And what had she done? She had screamed and yelled and carried on as if he were going to hurt her. Well, that's what he felt like doing now. His fists clenched. *Caitlin Ryan*. Grown-up and lovely, back in Rock Ridge after all these years.

Furious, he wanted to pull her to her feet, drag her outside, and expose her to everyone.

But he hesitated.

He couldn't do it. The rational part of his mind stopped him. After all, his little sister was there with her. And Kathy adored her. She thought Caitlin Ryan was wonderful. If he did what he wanted, it would only hurt Kathy. His revenge would have to wait.

So, instead, he stood in the open doorway and called to his sister. "Kathy! Kathy, come here. We've got to go home now."

Caitlin and Kathy both looked up at once. But all that Caitlin could see was the shadowy outline of a tall young man. The light streaming into the room from behind him made it impossible to see his face. "Come, Kathy," he said. "Mama's waiting and we have to go now." He turned and left.

71

"Wait! Wait!" Kathy ran toward the door after her brother. "Don't leave yet. *Please!* I want you to meet my teacher."

But Jake was already out of sight. Kathy turned back to look at Caitlin, an expression of confusion and hurt on her face. "I'm sorry, I have to go now," she said in a small voice.

Caitlin could only shake her head. "It's okay, honey. Go ahead."

She didn't know what the problem was with Kathy's brother, but he certainly didn't seem to be a very nice person.

9

Caitlin finally decided that the time was right to reveal who she really was.

One afternoon when the mothers had gathered to pick up their children, Caitlin invited them into the school room. Fearfully, she stood before the mothers and explained who she was and her reasons for deceiving them.

"So," she finished, "I am really Caitlin Ryan. But I am also the same person you've come to know the last three weeks and, I hope, trust. I count you as my friends. And I very much want you to do the same."

For a long moment the room was silent. Then someone in the back muttered, "I mighta known. You just can't trust a Ryan."

Caitlin's heart sank. But then another mother hushed the dissenter and Jenny Sumney stepped forward to take Caitlin's hand in her own. Softly she said, "It don't really matter much what you call yourself, hon. We like you, anyway."

Soon the others were following Jenny's lead,

crowding around Caitlin, telling her that she was always welcome in Rock Ridge whenever she wanted to come.

As Jed told her later, "It looks as though you really won these people over. Even that woman who said something bad about you at the meeting came around eventually. Your grandmother should be proud of you. You've done a lot for the Ryan name."

Caitlin did feel good about the way most everything had turned out. But she did have one concern. Kathy Stokes had been absent the last week and a half, ever since the day she had tried to introduce Caitlin to her brother and he had left in such a hurry. She hoped it hadn't been because of anything she had done. And although she couldn't think of anything, she still worried.

When she asked some of the mothers about Kathy, they told her not to be concerned. The Stokeses kept pretty much to themselves because they lived so far out, the women said. But they also assured Caitlin that, if something really bad had happened, they would have known about it.

"More than likely Kathy's got a touch of summer fever," Jenny said. "You know how kids are. They'll eat something that's turned bad in the heat and have a stomachache for a few days."

Caitlin continued to hope that Kathy would return, especially for her and Jed's last day, because they had planned a farewell party.

Caitlin had had Mrs. Crowley bake a cake and a huge batch of cookies. And the children, with Emily's help, had made pretty paper flowers to give to the departing teachers. Emily and two of her friends were going to continue the school for another month. They had decided to try to make the summer school a project for each succeeding senior class at Highgate.

All during the party Caitlin kept looking at the door, half expecting to see Kathy's sunny, round face appear. But the party ended, and goodbyes were tearfully said. There was still no sign of Kathy Stokes.

"I'm worried," Caitlin told Jed as they were helping Emily clean and sort the supplies for the next session. "Suppose she's really sick. I'd feel terrible if she was and I hadn't done anything to cheer her up."

"Caitlin, stop worrying," Jed told her. "She probably just got tired of coming."

"For some reason I think I did something to upset her, to send her away. I can't leave Rock Ridge without knowing she's all right."

Jed put his hands on Caitlin's shoulders and said, "I'll go and check things out. You and Emily keep on organizing, and I'll see what the trouble is. Okay?"

"You don't mind?"

"Even if I did, I'd go to cheer you up."

Caitlin smiled up at him. "Well, I do wish I could see her myself. But I don't want to scare her off more. I'd like her to come back and attend the last month here if you can persuade her."

"I'll try. See you soon." Jed started for the door.

"Oh—wait a second," Caitlin called after Jed. "I nearly forgot. I brought something for Kathy."

Going over to her tote bag, she reached in and pulled out a beautiful doll. Its lovely hand-painted porcelain face and hands made it a collector's item. But from the way Caitlin was handling it, Jed knew it must have been a doll that had been greatly loved and a favorite of hers when she was little. "Tell Kathy her name is Bitsy." Caitlin carefully handed the doll to him. "And tell Kathy that she was very special to me when I was younger—and that I hope Bitsy will be just as special to her."

"I will." A lump had formed in Jed's throat that prevented him from saying anything more. Caitlin's gesture made him want to take her into his arms and tell her how special she was to him. He hesitated because Emily was watching. He turned and walked to the door. He would tell Caitlin just how touching he thought her giving the doll to Kathy was later—in private.

It took Jed nearly half an hour to find the Stokeses' cabin. It was at the top of a steep ravine, and the road leading up to it was full of potholes and muddy. He was glad that he had a four-wheel-drive car.

The small, weathered house with the sloping tin roof was almost hidden behind a small grove of scrub pines. He only saw it when he noticed a thin thread of smoke curling upward from the chimney. At least that meant that someone must be home, he thought. Although the houses in the area had electricity, many of the people still preferred to cook or heat in the winter with wood stoves, just as previous generations had done. He also noticed that one of the front windows was partially open. Surely whoever was in the house had heard him drive up, he thought. But no one came to the door.

As he approached, the only living creature he saw was a large, reddish dog lying in the middle of the dirt path. The dog raised his head, lifting one ear in Jed's direction. "Good boy," Jed said automatically as he walked around him and up the three steps to the sagging porch.

He knocked. Then he knocked again and finally heard someone moving around inside. But no one came to the door. This time he knocked a little louder. A moment later someone pulled back a part of the curtain at the open window. But whoever it was stayed hidden behind the curtain.

"Hello," Jed said. "Mrs. Stokes? Is that you?"

The curtain dropped back down.

Jed leaned close to the door and called. "It's Jed Michaels, Mrs. Stokes, from Project Acorn. I came to see how Kathy is—and to bring her something. From Caitlin."

He heard the sound of a latch being lifted. Before Jed had time to move away from the door, it was yanked open, and he found himself standing face-to-face with a young man a couple of years older than he was. Dark, flinty gray eyes stared at him with such hostility that Jed moved back onto the porch involuntarily.

"Umm—I—"

That was all Jed got out before he found himself being grabbed by the collar of his shirt and pulled forward. "Now you listen, Mr. Jed Michaels," the boy said between clenched teeth. "And you listen hard. We don't want anything from the Ryans. Not now, and not in the future. Do you understand?" Jed could feel the other boy's hot breath on his face.

"Hey, look!" Jed was overwhelmed by his own anger, and those two words were all he could manage to say. He was desperately trying to figure out what was going on.

"Stop fighting. Please," came a frightened voice from inside the house. Jed figured it must be Mrs. Stokes. "These people have been real nice to Kathy. I don't want you saying those things."

"Ma, just leave this to me," the young man responded, not taking his eyes off Jed.

"Look. I just want to give this to Kathy," Jed said, barely controlling his temper. He held the doll up so that the young man could see it. "It's just a doll."

At that, Jed heard Kathy's voice coming from inside. "Oh, let me see it. Please. Please! I want to see her."

"Caitlin asked me to bring it to you," Jed called out to her. "She wanted you to have it, Kathy. The doll used to be hers. She said to tell you it had been her favorite and that it was very special to her. She said she hoped you would feel the same—"

Suddenly the doll was ripped from his hand, and Jed was pushed away at the same time. He tripped backward down the three steps, barely keeping his balance.

What happened next nearly made Jed sick. Jake angrily smashed the doll against one of the porch posts. As he did, the delicate porcelain head shattered into thousands of tiny fragments, which rained down across the wooden porch.

"There!" Jake flung the headless doll out into the yard, where it landed beside the startled dog. "Take that back to your precious Caitlin Ryan."

"Just a second—" Jed started, but he was cut off as Kathy's brother ran down the steps at him. Jed raised his hands to defend himself.

But Jake landed the first blow. It hit the side of Jed's jaw, stunning him enough so that Jake could get in another punch, just below Jed's ear. Then Jed started to fight back.

The fight didn't last long. It wasn't so much that Jed was stronger than Jake, but that he wasn't as angry. He was calmer and planned his punches. And it was only moments before Jake was sitting on the ground, holding his head while blood streamed from his nose.

Jed stood staring down at Jake, his hands balled into fists at his sides. Hearing a sob from the direction of the porch, he looked up to see

Mrs. Stokes standing in the open doorway, her hands over her mouth and her eyes wide with fright. And behind her, Kathy's little round face peered out from behind her mother's skirt. Jed realized they had seen everything, and he felt a terrible pity for Jake.

Jed turned to walk away, promising himself he would never tell Caitlin about what had happened, nor would he let anyone else tell her—not if he could possibly help it.

Behind him, Jake rose unsteadily to his feet. He watched silently as Jed climbed into the Bronco and drove away. Then he swore softly, "Damn you, Jed Michaels. I'll get you. I'll get you no matter how long it takes, or how far I have to go—just the way I'm going to get Caitlin Ryan."

10

The long afternoon shadows were stretching over the back lawn at Ryan Acres as Caitlin and Jed stood on the terrace, holding glasses of mineral water that had just been served to them. They were talking quietly.

"I know I should feel more nervous," Caitlin said, "about telling my grandmother about the problems we found at Rock Ridge. But today has been so perfect, so relaxed." She smiled happily. "Just the two of us—alone together."

"I was beginning to feel as though I was sharing you with the entire world." Jed reached over to gently pull her toward him.

"Well, I suppose you might call Rock Ridge a world of its own." Caitlin became quiet and then said thoughtfully, "We did do some good there, didn't we? I'd hate it if those people felt we'd just been interfering in their lives."

"Don't you remember how those mothers threw their arms around you and hugged you when it was time to leave yesterday?"

"Yes. But we could have and should have

81

done more. And I'm feeling sorry for myself that I didn't get a chance to say goodbye to Kathy." She sighed deeply, then smiled at him. "But I'm glad you did—and made sure she was all right. I'm really happy she liked the doll so much."

"She loved it!" Jed had to turn his head as his throat closed on the lie. How he hated to lie to Caitlin that way. But it was certainly better than the alternative. If he could help it, she would never discover the horrifying truth.

"And you told her the doll's name was Bitsy?"

"Yes—yes, I did," Jed replied, managing to keep his voice even.

"Jed"—Caitlin touched his shoulder—"is there something that you're not telling me?"

Forcing himself to look happy and unconcerned, Jed turned to Caitlin. "No, nothing's wrong." He shook his head and managed to smile. "I was thinking about what we're going to be discussing with your grandmother after dinner. You know, trying to organize the facts—that kind of thing."

"Well, now that you've brought—" Caitlin stopped in midsentence as Rollins stepped out onto the terrace.

"Excuse me," he said apologetically. "But Mrs. Ryan has arrived home and has requested your presence in the living room. And I am to tell you that dinner will be served shortly."

"Thank you, Rollins," Caitlin said. Turning to Jed, she put her hand in the crook of his elbow. "As I started to say, now that you've brought it up, I'm beginning to feel those nerves that I said

I wasn't feeling a few minutes ago." She took a deep breath. "Shall we go in?"

Mrs. Ryan was waiting for them, a martini in her hand. Because she had stayed late at the office, there was only time for a brief discussion of how Jed and Caitlin had spent the day.

There was an unwritten but strictly enforced rule that business of any kind was never discussed during meals. So, the three of them continued to keep the conversation light through the chilled soup, the herbed chicken breasts served with wild rice and baby carrots, and the chocolate mousse for dessert.

Finally Mrs. Ryan rose, suggesting that they go into the library for coffee. If someone had asked Caitlin when she was leaving the table what they had talked about, she couldn't have answered.

Settled in the lovely book-lined room, the Paul Revere silver coffee service gleaming on the low Queen Anne table between them, Mrs. Ryan looked over at Jed and Caitlin.

As she did, Caitlin felt like a child. She was perched on the edge of the sofa, just the way she used to when she was little and had been allowed to stay up late enough to tell her grandmother what she'd done that day before being taken up to bed by her nurse. She blinked hard, trying to concentrate on the present.

"Well, now," Mrs. Ryan said as she poured from the silver pot and handed a cup to Jed, "Caitlin mentioned that you both wanted to discuss something about Rock Ridge with me."

She smiled graciously. "About Project Acorn, I gather." She poured for Caitlin, then for herself, adding one cube of sugar to her own cup and one to Caitlin's. "From what I've heard, it's a tremendous success."

"I think it is, Mrs. Ryan." Jed set his coffee cup down. "However, that's not what we want to talk to you about." Reaching into the inside pocket of his jacket, Jed withdrew a packet of papers. He unfolded them, then pushed the coffee service aside just enough so that he could spread the neatly typed pages out in front of her. "While we were there, we happened to discover some problems that have to do with the mine. Safety problems."

"Safety problems?" Mrs. Ryan seemed to stiffen, squaring her narrow, patrician shoulders. "What could you two possibly know about safety problems? They are handled by mining engineers. And Ryan Mining has an excellent one."

"Caitlin"—Jed turned to her—"do you want to start?"

As Jed had been talking, Caitlin had been hardening her determination, thinking about the lined faces of the miners' wives she had spoken to over the past few weeks.

"Yes, of course." Her voice was strong. "We know quite a bit about the safety problems, Grandmother. Not so much as a professional engineer, I grant you. But what we learned, we learned from the people who work in the mine. And I think that makes them experts as well.

And from what we learned, I think there are some things that need to be looked into."

"Such as?" Mrs. Ryan folded her slender hands in her lap. Caitlin noticed her grandmother's gesture and smiled to herself. It was an unconscious gesture her grandmother did whenever she prepared to really listen to someone.

"Well, basically it boils down to two major problems," Caitlin began. Together, she and Jed explained all of the safety problems their research had uncovered.

When they had finished, Mrs. Ryan was nodding. "Yes. Yes, I see." Slowly she reached out and picked up one of the pages. She studied it, and after a few minutes, she looked up at Jed. "Are you really certain these figures are accurate?"

But just as Jed was about to reply, they were interrupted by a voice from the doorway. "Certain of what?"

All three turned their heads. Colin Wollman, looking poised and assured, one hand thrust casually into the pants pocket of his expensive beige summer suit, stood in the open doorway.

"Colin!" Regina Ryan sounded both surprised and delighted. "I thought you weren't going to be back from Washington in time to stop by. Do come in and sit down. I'll ring for some fresh coffee. Besides, I want you to hear what Caitlin and Jed have just brought to my attention— some rather disturbing facts about the safety of the mine at Rock Ridge."

"All right." He smiled confidently. "I'd be glad to hear what they have to say." He crossed the room in long, easy strides, then sat down on a chair near Mrs. Ryan. After unbuttoning his jacket, he sat back and smiled again at Caitlin, then at Jed. "Now, I really am very interested in hearing what you have to say about Rock Ridge. I know I've been with the company only a short time, but I'm quite familiar with that particular site."

"Well, it's as I just finished telling—"

"Oh, excuse me, Caitlin." He held up his hand to stop her from talking further. "Just a moment." He turned to her grandmother. "Did you say you were going to ring for fresh coffee? I just drove all the way from Washington, and I'm quite tired."

"Yes, of course, Colin," Mrs. Ryan said quickly, reaching for the little silver bell on the tray. She rang it. Almost immediately the maid appeared in the doorway. "Margaret, would you be so kind as to bring some fresh coffee and another cup for Mr. Wollman." She turned to him. "Would you like a sandwich, or something else to eat?" He shook his head, murmuring, "No, thank you."

"All right, then." She looked back at the maid. "Just the coffee, Margaret."

"Yes, ma'am." There was a pause as the maid retrieved the silver pot and took it away to the kitchen to be refilled.

While Margaret performed her task, Caitlin watched Colin's face. It was obvious to her that he wasn't the least bit interested in hearing what she and Jed had to say. She could tell from his superior expression that he had only agreed to listen in order to please her grandmother. When Caitlin realized this, every uneasy or bad feeling she had ever felt about Colin Wollman surfaced, and her stomach tightened in a hard knot. She glanced at Jed. Did he realize what was happening?

"Now, then, Caitlin"—Colin's smooth voice interrupted Caitlin's thoughts—"why don't you repeat for me what you told your grandmother." But, as Caitlin began to explain again what she and Jed had discovered, she noticed that Colin wasn't really paying attention to what she said. He smiled as though she were telling him about a sand castle she and Jed had built in their sandbox. At one point he became so absorbed in removing a small piece of lint from his trousers that Caitlin stopped speaking for a moment. He didn't even notice. Finally she went on with her description of the miners' safety problems, but her story had lost all the energy and conviction it had had when she'd told it to her grandmother.

"Very interesting, very interesting," Colin said in an approving tone when Caitlin was finished. He put down his coffee cup and leaned over the coffee table, shuffling the typed pages around haphazardly. *He certainly isn't looking at them very carefully*, Caitlin thought.

After a few minutes Colin sat back. Mrs. Ryan, eager to hear his opinion, said, "Well, Colin, tell me what you think. What about the fan out at that mine? And what about the other problems they have come up with? You know how I insist on operating strictly within government regulations, but these figures—" She tapped the reports with a beautifully manicured fingernail. "These figures indicate that their standards just aren't enough. And especially if that fan is continuing to break down—as Caitlin says."

"Well, first of all, before I answer, let me compliment these two young people on their report. It's very commendable—very commendable, indeed." As Caitlin listened to his patronizing tone of voice, she could feel the knot in her stomach grow tighter. She wanted to reach over and scratch that confident look off his face. Instead she sat, absolutely still, as he explained away every bit of evidence she and Jed had painstakingly put together. By the time he had finished, she was almost ready to believe him herself. But she didn't because she knew she and Jed were right.

"So you see," he said, winding up with a smile directed at both Caitlin and Jed, "the problems all sound serious, but they aren't really." He turned to Regina. "You should know that if there were any safety hazards at Rock Ridge or at *any* of the Ryan mines, I would have taken care of them as soon as I started. And I had a careful inspection made of each site before I agreed to be your attorney. I know for a fact that all Ryan Mining operations are safe." He paused for a moment before going on. "I do admire your granddaughter and her friend for their concern. But, simply put, there aren't really any problems."

Caitlin wanted to scream. Instead, she looked at her grandmother. Mrs. Ryan was totally captivated, both by the speech and the man.

Caitlin wasn't at all surprised when her grandmother said, "I'm sorry, dear, but I'm afraid Mr. Wollman has a point. He is in a position to see the whole picture, while you and Jed saw only a small part." To ease the sting of her words, she smiled and put her hand on top of their notes. "But he is right in commending the excellent job you two did. And I hope you'll continue to show as much concern about Ryan Mining in the future—especially once you've started your business courses at college."

"Yes, Grandmother," Caitlin replied. She was smart enough to know that any further attempt to discuss the matter would just make things worse. "Thank you for listening."

Averting her eyes from Colin Wollman, she stood up. "Jed, I guess we should leave my grandmother and Mr. Wollman alone so that they can discuss *business*." It wasn't much, but her harsh remarks gave Caitlin a tiny bit of satisfaction. And it was about as angry as she dared to get under the circumstances.

Jed had stood up when Caitlin had. After saying a polite good night to both Mrs. Ryan and Colin Wollman, he followed Caitlin from the room. As soon as they were out of earshot, he turned to face her. She had a furious look on her face.

"Do you believe that man!" she hissed. "Now—now do you see what I mean about him?"

"Yeah." Jed nodded solemnly. "I sure do. And I'm sorry, Caitlin. I really thought we had your grandmother convinced." He put his hands on her shoulders. "But don't give up hope. Maybe later on you can talk to her again."

"Oh, don't you worry about my giving up, Jed." Caitlin's eyes narrowed. "I'm not the type to do that." She shook her head with determination. "Don't you worry!"

11

For a couple of days Caitlin fumed about the put down she and Jed had gotten from Colin Wollman. But as the date drew nearer when she was to leave for Montana, she turned her thoughts to the trip. Colin Wollman and the problems at the mine would just have to wait until she got back.

To get herself ready, she spent one afternoon going through her clothes and spreading the ones she was going to take over her bed and chaise longue. After studying the selection she decided that a shopping trip was definitely in order. She had very few clothes that would be appropriate in a rugged place like Montana. Fortunately, there were several good clothing stores in Middletown where she could buy most of the things she would need. She went to her desk, took out a pad and pencil, and sat down to make a list.

The next morning Caitlin tucked the list into her purse along with her credit cards. She was about to leave the house to drive into Middletown when one of the maids, Catherine, came in to tell her that there was a phone call for her.

"Thank you, Catherine," she told the maid. "I'll take it in the library."

"Caitlin, hello!" the warm voice of Dr. Westlake greeted her when she picked up the receiver. "Catherine said you were just on your way out. I hope I'm not keeping you from something."

"Father, hello!" Caitlin said in a happy voice. "No, you're not keeping me at all. I was just going into Middletown to do some shopping for my trip to Montana."

"Oh, I'm glad I caught you. I'm going to Middletown, too. I have a lunch date, and I was calling to ask if you'd like to join us—especially since you're going to be away for a month. This could be our last chance to spend time together until after you've gotten back. So what do you say? Do you want to have lunch with your old father—or are you going to be too busy buying out the stores?"

"You know I'd love to have lunch with you," Caitlin replied with delight. "Just tell me when and where."

"Well, how about the Chef's Inn? At one-thirty? Will that give you enough time to shop?" Dr. Westlake chuckled in a fatherly fashion.

"Plenty." Caitlin laughed back. "I'm just going to buy some jeans and maybe a pair of cowboy boots."

"Oh, I should have realized you wouldn't

need very many dresses in Montana," he replied. "Well, I'll see you at the restaurant. I'll wait in the lobby."

"And I'll just look for the handsomest man in the place," Caitlin answered. She smiled as she hung up the phone.

She looked down at the blue cotton jump suit she was wearing. It was perfect for shopping but nor for wearing to lunch with her father, so she decided to go back to her room and change. As she headed up the stairs, she remembered something her father had said on the phone—something about having a lunch date. She didn't think he'd ask her to join them if it were a business lunch. *It must be a woman*, Caitlin decided. She smiled. Whoever it was, her father must like her a lot to drive all the way from the hospital to see her.

Caitlin changed quickly. Picking up her purse and preparing to go back downstairs, she hoped her father's new lady friend was nice. He deserved to be as happy with someone as she was with Jed.

Dressed in a pink sleeveless linen dress, her dark hair pulled back from her face by a headband of the same color, she went down the outside steps to where Rollins held the door of her Nissan 280ZX for her.

"Are you sure you wouldn't prefer that I drive you in the Bentley, Miss Ryan?" Rollins offered. "You look so lovely, you really shouldn't have to drive yourself."

"Thank you, Rollins." Caitlin smiled warmly

at the portly man. "But it's much too lovely a day to be cooped up in the back of that big car."

"As you wish, miss." Rollins bowed slightly, then carefully closed the door of the sports car after Caitlin got in.

It was nearly quarter past one when Caitlin walked out of the last store, her arms loaded with packages. She had just enough time to go back to the parking lot and put her packages in the back of her car before meeting her father. The Chef's Inn was only two blocks from the car, and on her way she could look into the stores along the street.

After she had carefully locked her shopping bags away, she started to walk toward the main entrance to the lot when she noticed two people standing beside a black Jaguar, which was blocking the entrance. They were Nicole and Colin Wollman. As far as Caitlin was concerned, she had seen far too much of Colin Wollman lately. He was at Ryan Acres all the time now. Either that or he was escorting her grandmother to some party or business function. And as for Nicole, she could do without ever having to speak to her again.

Caitlin looked around at the back of the parking lot. She could leave that way, but it would take her longer to get to the restaurant because she would have to go through a little outdoor mall and then around another block.

Still, she would rather walk an extra block than say hello to Colin Wollman and his sister.

But just as she was going to turn around and head toward the back exit, she stopped and continued looking at the pair. Colin's actions toward Nicole didn't seem very brotherly. He was caressing her shoulder. And the expression on his face didn't seem to be the kind of look a brother would give a sister, either. It was as if they were lovers . . .

You're being silly, Caitlin told herself, shaking her head. Suddenly feeling embarrassed, she turned around and walked quickly toward the rear exit.

She arrived at the restaurant only a few minutes late. Her father was waiting for her just inside. Putting his arm around her shoulders, he gave her a quick squeeze. "I'm so glad you could make it, Caitlin. I already have a table, so we can go right in. I hope you don't mind that we're not having lunch alone."

Caitlin looked up into his handsome face with a twinkle in her eye. "You mean the date you mentioned over the phone?"

"Yes." He looked at her with a boyish grin. "And you know her. She thinks you are absolutely wonderful—just as I do.'"

Caitlin was thoroughly confused. She wondered who he could possibly mean. "Who is she?" she asked.

"Just wait, you'll find out," he assured her as he led the way through the maze of crowded tables. The popular restaurant was nearly filled, so it wasn't until they had almost reached their table that Caitlin finally saw who this mysterious woman was.

"Nicole Wollman—" Shocked, Caitlin couldn't think of anything else to say.

"You see," Dr. Westlake said to Nicole, "didn't I tell you she'd be thrilled?" Totally misinterpreting the stunned look on Caitlin's face, he turned to his daughter. "Here, honey," he said, pulling out a chair, "let me help you." Caitlin felt as if her knees were going to buckle backward. She quickly sat down.

"So, Caitlin"—Nicole's voice was all charm—"how nice to see you again. How have you been?"

"What?" Caitlin blinked. Nicole was acting as if they were close friends, although they had only spoken briefly at the party her grandmother had given for Colin. "I've been fine, thank you," she replied absently, trying to sort out her thoughts. "And you?"

"Oh, fine—just fine, dear."

The waiter arrived to take their order, interrupting the conversation for the moment. They all quickly scanned the luncheon menu while he waited. Dr. Westlake ordered the chilled seafood plate and white wine for himself and Nicole. He turned to Caitlin and asked what she would like. When she told him she wanted only a small salad and a glass of iced tea, he raised an eyebrow at her but passed the order on to the waiter. The waiter then picked up the menus and left.

"Shouldn't you be having something more than just a small salad and tea?" Dr. Westlake asked Caitlin. "You've been shopping all morning. I should think you'd be ravenous."

"Oh, Gordon. I'm sure she's like most girls her age," Nicole interjected, sounding as though she were on Caitlin's side, "concerned about her figure."

"But she has a perfectly lovely figure," Dr. Westlake replied. "In fact, if anything, she's a little on the thin side."

"Well, I remember how it was when I was Caitlin's age." Nicole smiled sweetly at Caitlin. "Every time I'd go shopping and look at myself in those dreadful three-way mirrors, I'd spend the next two days practically starving myself. Sometimes you don't realize how much baby fat you still have until you spend a day trying on clothes. Don't you think so, Caitlin?"

"I don't think I ever had baby fat," Caitlin replied evenly.

"Oh." Nicole nodded. "How lucky for you." She gave a light laugh, completely undisturbed by the cool way Caitlin was reacting.

Their lunch was served, and Dr. Westlake and Nicole discussed the tenderness of the crabmeat and the lightness of the sauce. Caitlin, having picked up her silver salad fork, pushed a spinach leaf back and forth on her plate and thought about Nicole. She still couldn't get over the way she and Colin had been acting toward each other in the parking lot. It had seemed as if they were in love with each other rather than loved each other as brother and sister. And now there Nicole was, sitting with her father, acting as if he were the only man with whom she could be romatically involved. Caitlin felt like looking Nicole straight in the eye and demanding to know just what was going on. But, of course, she couldn't do that. What would her father think?

Nicole, noticing the distant look on her face, turned toward Caitlin. "Gordon tells me you're about to leave for Montana for a month. That should be very lovely for you."

"Oh?" Caitlin glanced toward Dr. Westlake. "When did you tell her that?"

"Hmmm." Dr. Westlake put down his fork. "I don't remember exactly." He glanced fondly at Nicole and said, "Was it when we went to the theater the other night?"

"The theater!" Caitlin blurted out rudely before she could catch herself. So it was true! She was right when she had thought Nicole was acting like her father's lover. They were actually dating. Caitlin was repulsed by the thought.

"I'm sorry, honey," Dr. Westlake said, seeing what he thought was confusion on his daughter's face. "I guess I should explain. As you know, I met Nicole at the party for her brother, Colin. We got to talking and discovered we have quite a lot of interests in common. And, well, we've seen each other a few times since."

"Yes." Smiling, Nicole reached a slim hand across the tabletop and placed it over Caitlin's father's hand. "It started while the string quartet was playing the *L'estate* from *The Four Seasons* and I introduced myself to your father. You know, Vivaldi's *Summer* concerto." She looked at Caitlin.

"Yes," Caitlin barely kept from snapping. "I know the piece. So?"

"So"—Dr. Westlake took Nicole's hand in his—"it just seemed very fitting. And we discovered we both are fond of chamber music."

"Your father said he knew of a concert of Mozart pieces that was being presented in Washington the following Tuesday." She smiled tenderly at Dr. Westlake. "Well, Gordon asked me if I'd like to go, and, of course, I said yes."

"Of course you did!" This time Caitlin did snap. With an abrupt move, she pushed her chair back and stood up. Throwing her napkin onto the table, she said, "Excuse me. I'm going to the powder room" and left. She walked quickly through the crowded room and disappeared into the lobby.

Confused by Caitlin's rudeness, Dr. Westlake watched her go. Then he turned back to Nicole. "I'm sorry. I don't understand what came over her just now. The way she acted—that isn't like Caitlin at all."

"Oh, don't worry, Gordon," Nicole assured him, giving his hand a pat. "Your daughter is acting perfectly normally."

"That's normal?" Dr. Westlake shook his head.

"Now I really don't understand. You must know something that I obviously don't."

Nicole laughed lightly. "If you'd been a father a little longer, you'd know, too. I think she's just a little jealous, that's all."

"Jealous? Of you? But she's my daughter, and you're—"

"Just a good friend," Nicole finished smoothly. "Gordon, she's only seventeen—she's still a little girl in many ways. And little girls can be very possessive of their fathers—especially when they've only just found them."

"Do you really think that's all it is?" Dr. Westlake asked. "You don't think it's anything more serious?"

"Of course not," Nicole assured him. "If I thought it was anything serious, I'd have followed her right into the powder room to see if there was anything I could do."

He nodded. "That makes me feel so much better."

"And you wait and see. The next time the three of us are together, she'll come around." Nicole paused and lowered her eyes. "If there *is* a next time, that is."

"Oh, there definitely will be a next time." Smiling tenderly, he squeezed her hand. "That is, if I have anything to say about it. All I want right now is for you and Caitlin to really get to know each other and become friends."

* * *

In the powder room Caitlin sat in front of the mirror, clenching her teeth so hard they hurt. How could her father be so easily fooled by that—that creature? Why, she could see through Nicole as if the woman were made of glass. But as Caitlin looked into the fringed blue eyes reflected back from the dressing table mirror, she admitted to herself that she could see what Nicole was like because she'd been like Nicole once herself. She, too, had been a flirt and a schemer. But she also sensed that she had never been so ruthless as Nicole.

Well, Caitlin reasoned, at least she was able to see what was going on—that Nicole was playing games. And, although there wasn't much she could do about it, she would figure out a way to get Nicole Wollman out of her father's life. With renewed determination, Caitlin checked her makeup and hair. Satisfied that both were perfect, she picked up her purse and got ready to go back out and face the enemy. It was too bad that she would be leaving for Montana in two days. She didn't like knowing that Nicole would have the next month with her father. But there was nothing Caitlin could do. She would just have to put whatever plans she could come up with on hold until she returned.

12

The day Jed and Caitlin were to fly west finally arrived. Mrs. Ryan said goodbye to Caitlin just after breakfast, then hurried off to her office. An hour later, after Rollins had carefully stowed her four matching French suitcases into the trunk of the Bentley, they drove to Brookridge Farm, where they picked up Jed. Rollins then headed for the airport, which was just outside Washington, D.C.

Half an hour after Rollins had unloaded their luggage at the curb, Caitlin and Jed were walking through the accordian tube connecting the terminal building to the huge jet. Caitlin felt a thrill of anticipation about meeting Jed's family. She wasn't nervous, just excited. She felt confident, knowing that she looked her best in the soft pastel cotton knit dress she had bought just for the trip.

Caitlin had decided to carry a lightweight white wool jacket, in case Montana was chilly. Jed had assured her she wouldn't need it, but she decided to bring it anyway. She had it over her arm as she entered the first-class compartment. The flight attendant immediately offered to hang it up for her. She also took the clothes bag Jed was carrying.

"We'll be serving lunch in about an hour," the young woman told them. "And drinks will be brought around as soon as we're off the ground."

The plane took off, and the flight attendant brought them soft drinks as well as appetizers. Lunch turned out to be small, perfect steaks, served with tiny new potatoes brushed with butter and sprinkled with fresh parsley. Then a dessert tray filled with delicious-looking pastries was wheeled by.

"Ah, that was a great meal," Jed said after the last of the dishes had been cleared away. "I never can understand why people complain about food on airplanes."

"Jed, honestly! You know very well what they serve in coach—sandwiches or TV dinners." She paused and looked at him, her head tipped to one side. "You're kidding me, aren't you? I don't believe for a second that you've never flown coach."

"Okay, you're right." Jed grinned. "But the real question is—have you?"

"Well—"

"I didn't think so." Jed laughed.

"But I have. I have, too!" Caitlin insisted, leaning toward him. "You're trying to make me sound like a terrible snob. I was only trying to remember exactly when it was."

"So you have?"

"Yes." She nodded. "It was in Europe. France, I think—or maybe it was that time we went straight to Switzerland from Rome."

"I rest my case. Do you realize I've never even been out of the United States? Except to Canada, which doesn't really count. And here you are—a seasoned world traveler."

"Poor little underprivileged Jed," she teased.

"Not too underpriviledged," Jed said in a low voice. "I have you." As he spoke, the warm look in his green eyes grew more intense. Their faces were so close that she wondered if he would sneak a kiss. But as she wondered, the flight attendant interrupted them. She was handing out earphones, wrapped in individual plastic bags, for the movie.

Jed didn't try to kiss Caitlin again, but as the movie began, he reached over and took her hand. She smiled at him, and they both settled back to watch the movie.

The plane landed in Denver, and they then changed to another that would carry them to Billings, Montana.

In Billings they changed to a much smaller plane, which would take them to the small town of Yellowtail Ridge, about forty minutes from the Michaelses' ranch.

Since they were flying at a lower altitude, Caitlin was able to get her first real look at Montana. She saw stretches of grassland burned yellow by the summer sun, and rolling hills covered with green shrubs. Beyond that stretched row upon row of flat buttes, banded beige, red, yellow, blue, and purple. But it was the Rockies that drew her attention. The only thing she could think of that compared to their breathtaking snow-covered peaks were the Alps in Europe. And it was possible, she thought, that the Alps came in second.

"Oh, Jed," she said in a soft voice, her face against the window. "It's so dramatic. Virginia must have seemed so tame when you first saw it."

"Don't put Virginia down. It has a different kind of beauty. Believe me, when I first got there, I couldn't get over how much green there was. It really amazed me. I just couldn't imagine how any place could be so totally one color."

"You're right. And I love Virginia, too." Caitlin said, not taking her eyes from the view. "But out here, there's just about every color imaginable."

Jed leaned across her to point. "Hey, see that range of hills over there—that one that looks like a man lying on his back?" Caitlin nodded. "Our ranch is at the base of those hills. Well, at least the west range is."

"The west range?" Caitlin's eyes widened as she turned to Jed. "Just how big is your father's ranch? I know it's large, maybe twenty or thirty times as big as Ryan Acres. But you make it sound really huge."

"Actually, it's small as cattle spreads go

around here. The ranch is only a little over thirteen thousand acres. But because my dad is so efficient and because we raise a variety of beef cattle that needs very few acres to graze on, the small size isn't so important." Jed's voice was full of pride.

Over thirteen thousand acres, Caitlin repeated silently to herself. Leaning back in her seat, she looked at Jed, who was still staring past her at the hills below them. Suddenly she saw him with new eyes. Why had she never asked about the size of his father's ranch? And he had just told her his father bred an unusual variety of cattle. Why hadn't she known that before? The answer was simple—she'd never thought to ask. When it came down to it, she knew very little about him. She knew he had a younger sister and that his father had brought them up since Jed's mother had run off. She also knew that Jed missed the West enormously. A feeling of guilt lodged within her as she realized it hadn't been important to her to really know about his past life and his home. When they had talked, it was usually about her life—the way she had grown up, her problems with her grandmother, the schools she had attended. True, they had Highgate in common, but even that was really a part of her world.

They had never really discussed in detail his life before Highgate. *Oh, Caitlin, you idiot*, she told herself. *You've been so self-centered that you hardly know anything about one of the most important people in your life*. Suddenly she wanted desperately to ask Jed a thousand questions—about his home, his father, his sister, the friends he'd grown up with. She wanted to ask all the questions she should have asked during the past two years.

A small jolt brought her out of her thoughts as the pilot turned sharply to get ready to land. Well, she told herself as she buckled her seat belt, now she would have the chance to learn about Jed's life.

Looking to her left, she saw that Jed had taken his hat down from the overhead compartment, put it on, and fastened his seat belt. She studied his ruggedly handsome profile—so strong beneath the curved brim of the light gray Stetson—and felt a little thrill run through her. Jed Michaels loved her!

As the plane rolled to a stop and then turned to taxi toward the small, wooden terminal building, she made a solemn promise to herself. She would spend the next month learning everything she could about Montana, the ranch, and anyone who was important to Jed—now, or in the past. She was also going to do everything she could to prove to both Jed and his family that she could fit into ranch life.

13

Eve Towers downshifted the black Jeep Renegade to make the sharp turn into the private dirt road of Wildrock Ranch. Then she immediately shifted up again and jammed the toe of her stylish, eel-skin boot against the gas pedal, sending the rugged little vehicle leaping forward like a suddenly spurred horse.

By the time she reached the main ranch house a few minutes later, a two-mile trail of dust could be seen rising behind her into the bright Montana sunshine. She brought the Jeep to a halt, turned off the engine, and swung her long, jean-clad legs to the ground. Just then, the front door was opened for her by her best friend, Melanie Michaels. Jed's sister had been called by her nickname, Annie, until the past year when she demanded to be called by her given name.

"Hey, what's the hurry, Eve?" she called to the tall, pretty girl who was striding quickly toward the house. "Jed's plane isn't due for two more hours."

"I know, I know." Eve's rich drawl was a bit

breathless as she stamped her dusty boots on the planks of the porch before following her friend inside. "But I wanted to get your opinion on how I look. If you think I don't look all right, then I'll still have plenty of time to go back home and change."

"Since when do you look anything but terrific?" Melanie said flatly. She would have loved looking half as good as Eve did at her worst.

"I'm serious, Melanie," Eve said with a touch of irritation. "I haven't seen Jed since last summer. And you know how important first impressions are." Stepping to the center of the room, she spun in a circle. "Now I want you to tell me what you honestly think."

Melanie crossed her arms and eyed her friend critically. Eve was facing her again, one hand on her slim waist and one knee bent in a model's pose.

"Well?" Eve demanded.

"What do you want me to say? You look great!"

"Be specific. What about my shirt? It's new. I got it in town yesterday. The lady said this shade of turquoise almost matches my eyes. What do you think?"

"She's right. Satisfied?"

"How about my pants?" Eve did another quick turn. "Do you think they fit all right?"

"You really want the truth?"

"Of course," Eve said. But even as she spoke, a tiny scowl appeared. "What's wrong?"

"I think they're too tight. But when is that

new to you? And they certainly do show every-thing. That *is* what you want, isn't it?" Melanie paused, knowing what she was going to say next would make Eve angry. "But—don't you think that silver belt buckle you got for being rodeo queen last year is just a bit much?"

"No, I don't." Eve's voice was positive. "It lets people know who I am."

"By people, do you mean a certain girl from Virginia?" Melanie shook her head and laughed. "You never give up, do you, Eve?"

"Well"—Eve raised a tanned hand and pushed a lock of golden hair off her shoulder—"I thought it was a subtle way of telling her that I'm someone she's going to have to reckon with."

"Subtle!" Melanie threw herself down on the couch, which was covered in butter-soft natural leather. "That's about as subtle as a cattle stam-pede. Why don't you wear your rhinestone crown as well?"

"Don't be ridiculous," Eve said.

"I'm sorry. I was just kidding." Melanie looked up at Eve, who was still standing in the center of the room with her hands on her hips, her eyes narrowed just enough to indicate to Melanie that she had gone a bit too far. "Come on, Eve, don't get all upset. It isn't worth it. Here, have a seat." She gave a sigh of relief as the other girl walked to a roomy chair covered in a fawn-toned leather that matched the couch. As Eve sat down, Melanie asked, "Do you want a soda?"

"Okay," Eve replied.

"I'll be right back." Melanie jumped to her feet and headed for the door that led into the kitchen. A moment later she returned, handing one of the frosty cans to Eve. She walked back to the couch, sat down, and put her booted feet up on the large, maple coffee table. "Seriously, Eve," she said, "Jed seems to really like this girl. After all, he wouldn't be bringing her out here to spend a whole month with us if he didn't."

"Melanie, I went out with Jed long before that spoiled little snob ever laid eyes on him. The only reason we broke up was because he went off to Virginia, to that high-society school. She's all wrong for him. I just have to get him to realize that. Which might not be all that hard." The corners of her mouth turned up in a self-satisfied smile. "You know what they say about your first love—you don't forget her. All I need to do is kiss Jed once, and it'll be all over for that girl. She'll be but a pale memory to Jed."

Melanie shook her head. "Eve, I think you're the one who's the pale memory here. Remember last summer when he was home. Absolutely nothing happened between the two of you. I would prefer to see you with Jed, but I don't think there's a chance."

"Just *you* remember, Melanie Michaels," Eve said. "I was having that problem with Hank Strode. Remember, he just couldn't get it through his thick head that I didn't want to go out with him anymore, after Jed got home? He just kept hanging around until I thought I'd go crazy. And the worst of it was that he scared Jed off."

Melanie was not about to contradict Eve, although she knew the real reason Jed hadn't been interested in her the previous summer was that he was still crazy about Caitlin Ryan.

"But now that Hank's out of the way," Eve continued, "I just have to think of a way to get Jed to see that I'm much better for him than Caitlin. It's that simple." Her eyes glazed over with a faraway look, and she began drumming the side of her soda can with her fingernails.

Melanie knew to remain silent. She had been friends with Eve all her life and recognized when her friend was hatching a scheme. Soon, Eve would have thought of a surefire plan. And when, a few minutes later, Eve's mouth began to turn up in what could only be described as a catlike smile, Melanie knew that this time the plan had to be a real winner.

"I've got it, Melanie," Eve said. "It's absolutely perfect. And it's simple, too. That's what makes it so perfect. By the time we're finished with Caitlin Ryan, Jed will wonder why he ever even noticed her. And, at the same time, he'll realize how right I am for him." She shook her head, swinging her golden hair away from her face. "I'll be back where I belong—as the one love in Jed's life—"

"Excuse me, Eve," Melanie said, interrupting Eve's gloating, "but did you say *we*—as in, both of us?"

"Right!" Eve looked at her. "Because it's definitely going to take both of us to pull this off."

"Eve, listen, you're my best friend, but Jed's my brother."

"Don't be a wimp, Melanie." Eve's eyes narrowed. "You just finished saying you'd rather see your brother with me than with that society girl from Virginia. Well, here's your chance to back up your words." With that she stood up. "Now, come on. Let's get going. I'll tell you all about my plan on the way to the airport. I don't want to be late for Jed's plane."

"You mean Jed and Caitlin's plane, don't you?" Melanie reminded her as she rose. "As of right now, they are still very much a couple."

"Ah, but that," Eve said, grinning wickedly, "is just a temporary situation."

14

As Caitlin stepped down on the portable steps that had been wheeled up to the plane, a gust of wind whirled across the landing field, sending dust twisting into the air and showering down in a fine layer over her. Throwing up a hand to shield her face, she waited until it had passed, then glanced over at Jed. He didn't seem to have noticed. Caitlin was annoyed, but she decided not to mention it. "I certainly hope that wasn't a sample of that western hospitality you promised me."

But Jed didn't hear her. She wasn't sure if it was because of the noise around them or because he was busy scanning the crowd of people behind the chain link fence to one side of the small, almost windowless, terminal building. Judging from the number of people standing there, Caitlin decided it must be the best spot to wait for arriving friends and relatives.

All at once Jed started yelling, "Melanie! Hey, Melanie, hello!" Then he grabbed Caitlin's hand and practically dragged her down the steps. It was all Caitlin could do to maintain her balance while she tried to juggle her carry-on bag, her purse, and her jacket. She was also having trouble keeping the clothes bag Jed had slung over his shoulder from knocking her purse out from under her arm.

"Jed, honestly!" she protested, once they had made it to the bottom of the steps in one piece.

She had finally gotten Jed's attention, and he turned around, giving her a brief, but sincere, look of apology. "Oh, Caitlin, I'm sorry. It's just that—well—" He gave her an abashed grin. "That's my sister!" Then he waved again and pointed. "See, that girl over there? The one with the tan hat."

Caitlin looked. Just about every person standing behind the chain link fence was wearing a hat, and half of the hats could be considered tan.

"Jed!" She raised her voice so he could hear her. "Which one?"

"The one waving. Don't you see?"

"Jed! Half the people over there are waving. And at least that many are wearing tan hats. Which one?" She was getting exasperated.

"Oh, sorry," Jed apologized. He gave an embarrassed laugh. "I guess I'm just excited."

She nodded.

"Okay." He leaned down so his mouth was close to her ear. "She's the one in the blue gingham blouse. Oh, now she's taken her hat off and is waving it over her head. You see her now?"

"Oh!" Caitlin smiled. "Of course." She had

spotted Melanie and could easily tell that she was Jed's sister. In fact, if she hadn't already known that Melanie was a year younger than he was, she would have mistaken them for twins. They both had the same light brown, wavy hair, the same strong face, and the same athletic build. The only difference was that Melanie was smaller and more feminine.

"Oh, Jed, she looks just like you. Now I know I can't help but like her. I—"

But once again, it was as if she were talking to air. A look of surprise had suddenly registered on Jed's face. "Well, I'll be *darned*." And before Caitlin could say a thing, he said, "Come on. Let's go inside. See, they're already starting toward the side entrance to the terminal."

They? she wondered as she followed Jed.

When they entered the building, she could see there was only one main room. It wasn't large, and in spite of the crowd, she could easily see the girl in the blue gingham blouse come bursting through the far door and run toward them. "Jed! Jed, oh, Jed!"

Jed, seeing her coming, stopped and dropped his clothes bag to the floor beside him. He held his arms open so she could throw herself into them, and he lifted her easily. Swinging her around in a circle, he kissed her soundly on the forehead before setting her gently back on her feet.

Then he looked past her, at the tall, slim girl waiting just a few steps behind. As they exchanged looks, the girl raised a slender, tanned hand and removed her hat, allowing a heavy mane of golden curls to cascade over her shoulders. Stepping forward, she reached her arms up to put around Jed's neck. "Welcome home, Jed," she said and rose on her toes to kiss him directly on the mouth.

It had all occurred so unexpectedly that Caitlin was still standing there telling herself the whole thing wasn't happening when Jed reached up to untangle the girl's slender arms from around his neck. Firmly but kindly, he separated himself from her. "Eve," he said, stepping back and turning to Caitlin, "I'd like you to meet Caitlin Ryan. Caitlin, this is Eve Towers, a friend and neighbor of ours." Moving to his sister's side, he put his arm around her shoulders. "And this, of course, is my sister, Melanie."

Her composure back, Caitlin extended her hand. "Hello, Melanie. I've been looking forward to meeting you." As they shook hands, Caitlin felt her strong grip and the calluses at the top of her palm. She remembered that Jed's hands had felt that way when she had first met him, too.

Managing to maintain the same smile, though it had definitely lost its warmth, she turned toward Eve. "Very nice to meet you, too, Eve." Jed had told Caitlin that he had once dated a girl named Eve. Caitlin knew that, from his point of view, it had never been serious. But Eve didn't seem to feel the same way.

The girl looked directly into Caitlin's eyes and said evenly, "Hello, Caitlin." Then she smiled. But there was no sign of welcome in her eyes at all. Despite the warm closeness of the filled room, Caitlin felt a chill go up her spine.

"Hey," Jed asked, excited to be home, "are we going to stand here all day, or are we going to get moving? I, for one, would love to get home and settle in." He smiled at Caitlin. "And I'm sure Caitlin feels the same way."

"I'm sorry," Melanie said. "Let's go get your luggage. The pickup's parked right out front."

"Pickup?" Caitlin wondered aloud. "Will we all be able to fit in?"

"Sure," Melanie assured her. "It's a king cab. There's one of those little seats behind the main one."

"I'll sit there," Jed said. "You three girls can have the front—"

"Don't be silly, Jed," Eve broke in. "You're wearing your city clothes. You sit in front with Melanie and Caitlin." She smiled at Caitlin, and for a second Caitlin was caught off guard enough to wonder if she had been wrong about Eve. "I'll sit in the back by myself."

Once they had stowed the luggage in the bed of the truck and climbed in, Caitlin realized why Eve had so kindly offered to sit in the uncomfortable rear seat.

With Jed sitting in the middle and Melanie driving, it was very natural for Eve to lean over Jed's shoulder to talk to him. As they drove away, she immediately started filling him in on all the local gossip. By the time they had reached the outskirts of Yellowtail Ridge, Caitlin noticed Eve's hand was resting lightly on Jed's shoulder. And, with Eve's head between Jed's and Melanie's, it was quite clear to Caitlin that she was purposely being excluded from the conversation.

She pretended to be interested in what the three of them were talking about, although the names and the places meant absolutely nothing to her. A couple of times she asked a question, but each time Eve smoothly changed the conversation to exclude her. Caitlin was fairly sure that Jed had no idea what Eve was doing, so although she wanted to say something, she didn't. It would have made her look petty in Jed's eyes. So, instead, she gritted her teeth and pretended to be completely absorbed in the view out the window.

She'd noticed that as they had been driving west, they had also been going up a gradual hill. The yellow of the flat grasslands had given way to gray-green, low, scraggly bushes. Caitlin decided it must be the sagebrush she had heard so much about. She turned to ask Jed about it, but he was still listening with rapt attention to Eve's gossip. Sighing, she turned away again.

Soon the road turned abruptly, and they were driving along a ridge but still climbing. Pines started to be mixed in with the sagebrush. A few minutes later, though, the pines became mixed with another variety of tree, whose slim white trunk and bright green leaves reminded her of the birches that grew in the wooded sections of Ryan Acres. They were pretty, and the leaves rustled with the slightest breeze. For a brief moment she had a flash of homesickness for the different green that was found in Virginia and on the East Coast.

Perhaps her feelings were mirrored on her face because Melanie leaned forward briefly and told Caitlin, "Those are aspens. In the fall their leaves turn a bright yellow-gold. That's where the town gets its name. You know, Yellowtail Ridge."

Given the chance, Caitlin leaped into the conversation. "Really!" she said quickly. "You know I was just thinking that those trees remind me a lot of a kind we have back in Virginia. You remember, Jed, there in the woods behind Ryan Acres?" He was looking at her now. She smiled back sweetly.

"Yes, I remember," he said. Then he suddenly gave a little shake of his head and looked apologetic. "I'm sorry, Caitlin. I should be showing you things instead of listening to Eve's stories. Eve and I can catch up on everything later. I totally forgot my manners."

"That's all right, Jed," Caitlin replied graciously. "I understand. I probably would have done the same thing."

"Well it won't happen again, I promise." As his green eyes locked with hers, she told herself she didn't need to worry about Eve. Jed was all hers. He wasn't interested in Eve, except for what she had been telling him. Caitlin wanted to reach over and take Jed's hand, but she decided that it wouldn't be appropriate in the situation. She smiled warmly instead.

They had left the ridge of pines and aspen and were descending now into a wide, grass-covered valley. "Do you remember that line of hills I pointed out to you when we were in the plane?" Jed asked. Caitlin nodded. "Well, they're right over there." He pointed through the wind-shield, and she saw what he meant—that the hills beyond outlined the shape of a sleeping man against the clear blue sky. "That's our ranch down there."

She looked to where he was pointing, but she couldn't see any sign of buildings. There were only the dark purple shadows of the hills stretching out against a sea of golden grass. And dotting the grass, like so many tiny fleets of ships, were groups of grazing cattle. She shook her head. "Where?"

"Hmmm. I guess you can't really see the main house right now. But it's there, trust me. Down at the base of those hills. We'll be there in about fifteen minutes. Then you'll know it's real."

"It's just that it doesn't look as though anyone lives down there. It's a beautiful valley. But, well, it's kind of empty looking."

"That's only because you're used to being in the East where everyone's all crowded together into small spaces," Eve said. "Our ranch and the Michaelses' ranch are the only two in this entire valley."

Reaching the valley floor, Caitlin noticed barbed-wire fences stretching along either side of the road. It surprised her. Having grown up in the affluent horse country of Virginia, she knew only that barbed wire did terrible things to animals caught in its sharp metal spikes. But then she remembered that it was used in the West to contain cattle. Still it was a bit of a shock to see so much of it.

As they passed a dirt road, which turned off the main road at an angle, Eve casually told Caitlin that it was the road that led to the Towerses' ranch, the Rocking T.

Caitlin said nothing, but wondered if she was supposed to be impressed by what she saw. She wasn't. From what she could tell, there was nothing but a dirt road and a lot of grass. It couldn't begin to compare to Ryan Acres, with the mansion house, the huge barn, the tennis court–swimming pool complex, all the lush pastures divided so evenly . . .

"Our ranch is almost thirty thousand acres," Eve bragged. "And we run the best Herefords and angus around."

"Hey, just be glad that's not what we raise anymore," Jed suddenly spoke up. "If Dad hadn't decided to change over to Simmental, yours wouldn't be best." He turned slightly in the seat to include Caitlin in the friendly debate. "If you want to talk about breeding, I'll stack our *horses* up against the Towerses' any day. Just wait until you see our horses, Caitlin."

"I'll bet they're beautiful, Jed," Caitlin said enthusiastically.

"Oh, hah!" Eve nearly snorted.

"Listen"—Jed turned back to Eve—"I'll challenge Charge Account against your wimpy Mr. Bars anytime. Count would be over the finish line before Mr. Bars even got his hocks in gear."

He turned back to Caitlin. "You remember my telling you about Count, don't you?" She shook her head. "Well, he's from racing quarter stock, and he's *really* fast."

"Hey, mister," Eve said, tapping on Jed's shoulder. "Would you like to put that in writing? Like on an entry blank for the race at the county fair? It's coming up in a few weeks. You'll still be here, won't you?"

"Yes. We'll see about the race, though." Jed laughed. "I want to talk it over with Count first."

"Ah-hah!" Eve raised the hand that was on Jed's shoulder and used it to punch him lightly. "Trying to weasel out of it already? You just know that Mr. Bars is a better horse and you won't admit it!"

"Here we are!" Melanie announced, putting an end to the mock argument. Slowing the truck, she made the turn onto a dirt road.

To Caitlin the driveway looked exactly like the one leading to the Rocking T. She was somehow disappointed. She wasn't sure what she'd expected—something grander maybe. She suddenly realized she had never actually visualized, in a realistic way, how Jed's father's ranch would look. She had had only a vague picture of something that resembled South Fork from "Dallas" on TV. A dirt road, with a huge mailbox beside it, didn't seem the least bit impressive. But, she had to remind herself, she was in Montana, not on a set for a make-believe Texas oil tycoon. And it was also not Virginia. You don't close off thirteen thousand acres with a white picket fence.

The setting sun was now in her eyes, so Caitlin still couldn't tell what the ranch house actually looked like. Then the truck passed into the shadow of the hills, and there it was, a little over a half mile straight ahead. They drove the distance in silence.

"So, what do you think?" Jed asked anxiously as Melanie brought the pickup to a halt.

From the sound of his voice, Caitlin could tell just how much he really wanted her to like his home.

Her first impression was that the house dominated the site at the base of the mountain, not the other way around. It was as though the house had been built first, then someone had decided the mountain might make a nice backdrop. The basic structure was long and low, made of redwood and glass. It had a main section and a wing at either end. The wings had been built at slight angles, which made them look as though they were bracketing the wide graveled parking area. Caitlin counted no fewer than five stone chimneys.

About eight hundred feet from one side of the house stood another structure. It was built of logs, with paddocks made from pipe. The barn was very different from the white colonial one at Ryan Acres, yet it wasn't any less imposing. There were other buildings as well, forming a complex that had a certain rugged handsomeness, especially since there was no purely decorative design or artificial landscaping. She smiled. The ranch was a little like Jed himself.

"Does that smile mean you like it?" Jed asked.

"I love it!" She smiled up at him. "I'm so glad I came."

"So am I," he replied in a low voice meant only for her. It made her feel as though he had just taken her in his arms and kissed her tenderly.

She was so caught up in looking at everything that she didn't see the flash of jealous anger in Eve's eyes or the look she gave Melanie.

"Hey, Jed," Melanie said. "I thought you were anxious to get into the house so you could settle in. Or have you decided that now that you've gotten this far, you'd prefer the front seat of the pickup to the living room? I mean, I could go get a couple of sodas, maybe even bring out the battery TV—"

"Okay, Melanie." Jed grinned. "I get your message loud and clear." He punched her leg in a brotherly way. "Have you got a hot date or something?"

"Look! It's a long way to town and back. I'd like to park the truck and go inside and relax. And, besides, Eve's still trapped in the seat behind you. Remember?"

Jed turned back to look at Eve. "Oh, I'm sorry. I forgot you were back there. I guess you want to get out, huh?"

Eve nodded sweetly.

Leaning across Caitlin, he pushed down on

the door handle so that the door swung open. "After you."

Caitlin swung her legs out, but stepping down from the high cab of the pickup was awkward in her high-heeled sandals. Jed had to lean over and catch her elbow to keep her from stumbling.

As Jed slid out to stand beside her, she felt awkward and clumsy and hated knowing that it was her own fault. She was angry when she noticed the practiced ease with which Eve slid from the truck, jumping lightly down to the ground.

"Well, guess I'll be leaving," Eve said. Briefly touching Jed's arm, she looked at Caitlin at the same time. "Nice to have you with us. I really hope you enjoy your stay." Before Caitlin could say anything in reply, Eve quickly returned her gaze to Jed. "See you later, Jed," she said, her voice dropping to a honey-soft drawl. Then, giving a little wave, she ran lightly over to where her Renegade was parked and swung gracefully up into the seat. She started the engine and, tires spinning in the gravel, sent the Jeep flying down the drive.

Watching the dust rise into the air behind the Jeep, Caitlin was very glad the girl had gone, but she hated her for her dramatic exit. As she turned back to face Jed, she suddenly realized how tired she was.

"Jed, I'm really sorry, but I'm exhausted. Would you help me get my luggage out of the back of the truck so I can unpack?"

"Sure," Jed agreed hastily. He looked solicitously at Caitlin. "I'll tell you what. Why don't I bring in your luggage while Melanie shows you to your room." He glanced at Melanie. "Okay?"

"Of course." Melanie smiled at Caitlin. "Come on. I think you'll like the room. Jed told me to give you the one that looks out on the valley." They mounted the wide redwood steps. Caitlin paused so that Melanie could open the massive, hand-carved front door. "It's got a great view," Melanie rattled on, but Caitlin was no longer really listening. The rooms they passed through were only a blur of comfortable, oversized leather furniture, colorful wool rugs on the polished plank floors, and beautiful paintings of western landscapes on the walls. All she wanted to do right then was to take a hot bath and curl up in a comfortable robe for a nap.

After they had reached Caitlin's room, Melanie showed no signs of ending what was almost nervous chatter. Caitlin finally had to say, "I'm sorry to be so impolite, Melanie. I really do look forward to sitting down and talking with you. Honestly. But, right now, I just want to change out of these clothes and lie down for a while." She glanced down at her dress, realizing with dismay how dusty it had become since she had gotten off the plane. "And take a bath. I feel really filthy."

"Oh, I'm sorry! Of course." Melanie nodded quickly. "Of course you want a bath." Then she shook her head. "Oh, I don't mean you look dirty. You look really nice. And I love that dress. But I know how grubby traveling can make you feel. Even though I've only been outside of Montana once—when we went to Denver for my cousin's wedding. It was—" She stopped, putting her hands over her mouth, while shrugging apologetically. "I'm sorry," she said again, dropping her hands back down. She pointed toward a door to one side of the spacious room. "The bathroom's over there. And there's a walk-in closet. And the drawers in the dresser have new scented paper in them. I hope you like the bed. It's not too soft. And it's not too— Oh, here comes Jed with your luggage."

Caitlin let out a long sigh when Melanie finally left the room and Jed came in. He was loaded down with all four of Caitlin's bags.

After setting them down, he stood looking at her for a long moment. "God! I can't believe you're finally here. Just think, Caitlin Ryan in Montana." With one finger, he pushed up the brim of his hat, then strode over to where she stood and gathered her into his arms. "I love you, Caitlin," he said softly. "Do you know that?" He gave her no chance to answer. His mouth came down over hers in the start of a long and tender kiss.

15

Caitlin awoke from her half hour nap feeling much better. Having already bathed, she changed from her light cotton robe into fresh linen pants and a simple cotton knit top. She brushed her hair until it hung, shining, to her shoulders. She felt self-assured once again. She was glad that Eve had left, if only for the evening.

As she walked out into the living room to meet Jed's father for the first time, she told herself she would do her best to win him over. Remembering how Melanie had tried, if not very hard, to include her in the conversation during the drive out to the ranch, she was fairly sure Jed's younger sister liked her. Now she just needed to prove to Mr. Michaels how right she was for Jed.

They immediately went into the dining room and sat at the massive dinner table to eat a meal of roast beef, mashed potatoes, biscuits, corn on the cob, and string beans—a meal obviously meant to satisfy a hardworking ranch owner.

Caitlin soon realized that Mr. Michaels wasn't that much different from any other business-man. Business was business, whether you sold cattle or coal. So, it wasn't very difficult for Caitlin to find the right questions to ask him to show her interest. After all, she had learned the fine art of dinner conversation from an expert—her grandmother.

When they had finished the last of the home-made blueberry pie, Jed suggested to Caitlin that they take a walk, perhaps down to the stable so he could introduce her to Count. But Mr. Michaels had other plans for Jed. "Sorry, son." He smiled kindly in Caitlin's direction. "I'd kind of like to monopolize Jed for this evening." He turned to Jed. "You and I have a lot of catching up to do. And there's some ranch business I'd like to get your opinion on." He turned back to Caitlin. "I hope you'll excuse this bit of fatherly selfishness."

"Of course," Caitlin replied. "Actually I'm still a bit tired from the trip. If you don't mind, I'd like to go to sleep early."

As they all rose from the table and Mrs. Mallory, the ranch housekeeper and cook, came in to clear away the dessert plates, Mr. Michaels asked her to bring coffee to the den for him and Jed and a pot of hot chocolate to Caitlin's room.

Jed told his father he would be right back. Then he walked Caitlin to her door. "I'm really sorry," he apologized. "But I can't say no to my father. Not on my first night home."

"I wouldn't want you to," Caitlin replied. She

put a hand up and ran it softly along the top of his shoulder. "I love you for caring."

"And I love you for being so understanding." He put his hands around her waist and drew her gently toward him. "Also I know you're really tired, so sleep in as late as you want in the morning, okay?" Then, bending his head, he gave her a tender good night kiss.

A few minutes later, after Caitlin had already put on a pale blue batiste nightgown and matching robe and was brushing out her hair, she heard a soft knock on her door. She opened it and found Melanie standing there.

"Hi." She greeted Caitlin almost shyly. "I'm sorry, but I couldn't help overhearing Jed tell you to sleep in late. Well, I thought you'd like to know—because I figured you'd want to make a good impression on my dad—that breakfast is at eight o'clock."

"Oh." Caitlin nodded. "Thank you, Melanie. Actually, I was going to ask when you usually eat breakfast. Jed was being nice, but I'd like to get up with everyone else." She put a hand on Melanie's arm. "Listen, I really appreciate your telling me. I want to make a good impression." She smiled. "Thank you for being a friend."

"That's okay," Melanie replied with a little shrug. "I like you." Then, as if she had said too much, she quickly turned and left, presumably down the hall in the direction of her own room.

* * *

The soft buzz of Caitlin's travel alarm sounded at precisely seven-fifteen the next morning. Reaching over, Caitlin flipped it off, gave herself a minute to come fully awake, and then sat up and swung her legs over the side of the bed. She stretched her slender arms over her head, ruffled her hair, and headed for the bathroom to shower.

Some five miles away, riding along a narrow trail at the base of the hills bordering the valley in which the ranch lay, Jed was guiding Charge Account past a clump of sagebrush. Behind him, about a mile back, Eve and Melanie were following, also on horseback. Eve had just cautioned Melanie, for the fourth time, to keep out of Jed's line of vision. As Melanie reined her horse back, Eve said, "So our little princess is still sleeping, huh?"

"Well, she was when I left," Melanie reported. "I did just as you suggested and told her the family always has breakfast at eight, instead of five-thirty. She'll get up thinking she's really going to score some points with Dad."

"And you're sure she believed you?"

"She's still asleep, isn't she?"

Eve gave a small laugh. "You know, that just proves how easy it's going to be to show her up for the tenderfoot she really is. Imagine anyone not realizing that, on a ranch, you have to get up early to get all the work done before the sun goes down. But, then, I don't suppose someone like Caitlin Ryan ever thinks about anything as mundane as work."

Melanie nodded. "But I'm not sure I can keep it up. Yesterday, when I first met her, I was so nervous just thinking about everything you told me you're going to do to make her feel out of place that I couldn't stop jabbering when I showed her to her room."

Eve shot her friend a scowling look. "You didn't spill anything, did you?"

"Of course not!" Melanie glared harshly at her friend. "What kind of an idiot do you think I am?"

"Well, okay." Eve's face relaxed. "So, we're on our way to making Caitlin feel out of place. By the time the two of us finish with her, she'll throw her designer clothes into her imported luggage and grab the first plane home." Eve gave a feline smile. "And Jed will be delighted to see her go. Because, by then, he'll have realized just how wrong she is for him."

"And naturally he'll realize that you're the right person for him."

"That's right!" Eve arched an eyebrow at Melanie. "Tell me. Do you think we should offer to drive the poor little tenderfoot to the airport?"

Melanie frowned. "Eve, you're not planning to pull anything more than just this kind of thing, are you? I mean, I don't want something really bad to happen."

"Don't be ridiculous, Melanie," Eve practically snapped. "Would I do something like that?"

"Well—"

"Never mind. And don't worry, there's nothing truly harmful about any of the things I've planned. Just stuff like this morning." Eve paused, and a slow smile spread across her face. "I wish I could see her face when she realizes that everyone's been gone for hours. And when Jed and I come riding in together, she's going to be furious."

"But we're not riding with him," Melanie reminded her. "Jed doesn't even know we're back here."

"Melanie, we're not just out here to trail him. I thought you knew that. When he starts toward home, we'll just casually ride up and meet him, and then we ride back together. And you fade into the background before we actually get within sight of the house." After all, there's no law that says we can't all be riding out here at the same time, is there?"

"Well—I suppose not," Melanie said. But she still wasn't sure she was doing the right thing by going along with her friend. Eve was her best friend, she had been for years, but Jed was her brother, and she didn't want to do anything that would make him unhappy. Yet, if it was true—as Eve had insisted—that getting rid of Caitlin would be the best thing for him, then she was all for that.

Caitlin was not back at the ranch, however. She had dressed and gone out to the kitchen expecting to find everyone at breakfast, but instead she had found only Mrs. Mallory, who was already slicing vegetables for the stew she would make for dinner. After she had said good morning, Caitlin asked Mrs. Mallory where everyone was. The cook had replied that they had all left hours before. Then she looked at Caitlin and smiled kindly. Young Mr. Michaels, she said, had gone toward the stables. Caitlin realized that Melanie had lied to her about the family breakfast time. Grabbing a bunch of grapes for her breakfast, she had gone outside to think.

As she had walked slowly down to the barn, thinking and eating the grapes as she went, she'd gone over everything that had happened the day before in her mind. Caitlin tried to figure out why Melanie would purposely lie the way she had. Then it all clicked: it was obvious that Eve was out to get Jed, and it was also fairly obvious that Melanie was Eve's best friend. And the easiest way Eve could get rid of Caitlin would be to make her look foolish in front of Jed. *Yes*, Caitlin thought, *that has to be it*.

"Well, sorry, Eve," she muttered aloud, "but you've just met your match. I'm not about to let you spoil this vacation for me." Throwing away the empty grape stem, she stuffed her hands into her back pockets and, with determined strides, set off toward the barn.

Caitlin managed to convince one of the stable hands that she knew what she was doing when it came to horses. A short while later, she was mounted on a husky bay, trotting along the trail that the stable hand had pointed out as the one Jed had taken earlier in the morning.

About half a mile from the ranch, the trail began to climb upward. Caitlin reached the top of the crest and was about to head down, when she noticed an interesting scene below. Jed was riding along by himself. Behind him, two riders had just spurred their horses into a canter and were racing toward him. But from the way he was riding, she knew he hadn't noticed them yet. And none of the three had noticed her. As the two riders approached Jed, coming closer to where she was at the same time, Caitlin recognized them. A smile spread across her face as she realized what Eve was up to.

Looking to her left, she saw that there was a shorter way down. Caitlin was sure that any horse on the Michaelses' ranch would be surefooted, so she took a chance and spurred her own mount, turning him off the trail and down the steep embankment.

Moments later she was safely reining up beside Jed, well before an astonished Eve and Melanie arrived.

"Hi, Jed." She smiled happily. "Just wanted to say good morning."

"Well, you sure did pick a great way of saying it!" A wide grin spread across his face as he pointed to the cloud of red dust rising from a shower of small rocks that were still cascading down the newly made trail. "And a very good morning to you, too." Then, leaning over in his saddle, he kissed her. They parted just as Eve and Melanie brought their horses to a halt beside them. The furious look on Eve's face made Caitlin's day.

* * *

Caitlin and Jed spent the next two days alone. He showed her around the ranch in the pickup and took her on a picnic to a lake back in the hills, where they swam and sunned and ate the huge lunch that Mrs. Mallory had packed.

Then, as Jed explained, it was time for him to do the work around the ranch that he was expected to do. "All right," Caitlin said. "But I don't want to be treated like a guest, either. I want to work as well." So she had spent the next week in the saddle, riding ten and twelve hours a day, helping Jed patrol all the fences bordering the property, stopping each time Jed spotted a place that needed mending. It wasn't long before she was handling the fence-mending tools as easily as he did.

One morning, a couple of days after they had finished the fence riding, Jed told Caitlin he wanted to teach her to shoot a rifle. Taking a twenty-two from the gun cabinet, he suggested they go down behind the stable where it would be safe to practice.

Jed lined up some empty tin cans along an old fence. Then he showed Caitlin the correct way to hold the gun, with the butt of the rifle solidly against her shoulder so that the muscle there would absorb the kick as the bullet left the barrel. Finally, he taught her how to line up both sights, the one at the end of the barrel and the one closer to her eye. "It's as simple as that," Jed explained. "As soon as you have your target lined up, gently squeeze the trigger."

Caitlin squeezed. The bullet cracked from the rifle. But the can she had been aiming at stayed firmly in place.

"Try again," Jed said with a smile.

She did. And this time the can flew into the air before falling to the ground.

"Great!" Jed exclaimed as she finished popping off the rest of the cans. As they both walked to the fence to set them up again, Jed explained why he wanted to teach her to shoot.

"Dad said I could have a couple of days off next week, and I thought we might take a trip up to Glacier National Park—maybe with the horses. It's a great place to ride, and I think you should see a real glacier before you go back to Virginia."

"You mean there are real glaciers in the United States?" Caitlin was completely surprised by Jed's statement.

"You bet." Jed's eyes twinkled. "About fifty of them—all in one park."

"So what am I supposed to do, shoot at one if it moves?" Caitlin asked, joking.

"Yeah, right." He smiled. But then his eyes turned serious. "The reason for the target practice is so that you'll know enough to be able to protect yourself. The park is pretty rugged where we'll be going, and we might run into a stray bear or mountain lion. I honestly don't think that's going to happen—they stay pretty far from the trails—but it never hurts to be careful. The last time I saw a bear up there was when I was about five."

Caitlin shot off the row of cans they had set up, then did it two more times. It turned out that she was one of those people who was a naturally good shot.

"Boy," Jed said, grinning, "I feel sorry for any bear that tries to cross you. You're a real natural. In fact, I think we ought to celebrate!"

"Celebrate?" Caitlin smiled happily up at him. "How?"

"Well, how about a good old-fashioned western barbecue—complete with a side of beef roasting over an open pit, Mrs. Mallory's famous sauce, and all the homemade beans you can eat?"

"That sounds fabulous. But all of that just because I can shoot a tin can off the top of a fence?"

"Actually, no." Jed wrapped his arms about her waist and pulled her to him. "As a matter of fact, I'd already planned a party for this weekend. I want you to meet my friends. And, more importantly, I want them to meet you. I want them to see for themselves what a terrific girlfriend I have."

16

On the night of the barbecue, Caitlin was in her room putting the finishing touches on her hair when people began to arrive. As she fastened her gold clip in place, the sound of the guests on the patio drifted through her open window. She stepped back from the full-length mirror to see how she looked. Caitlin was glad that she had packed her new silk jump suit, especially since Melanie had been kind enough to tell her that the embroidered western shirt and white jeans she had originally picked to wear wouldn't be appropriate. Even though it was only a barbecue party, she'd said, most of the guests would be wearing dressy clothes.

"I know that might seem kind of strange," Melanie had told her, "since it's a casual party and all. But out here, we wear jeans so often that we like to dress up whenever we have an excuse."

Caitlin smiled at her reflection, pleased with what she saw. The outfit, made of a heavy silk, the color of rich cream, complemented her black hair and new bronze tan. The wide gold belt made the outfit even dressier and emphasized her small waist. Yes, she thought, Jed would be proud of her as he introduced her to his friends.

As Caitlin left her room and made her way through the house to the patio, she thought of the party tapes she and Jed had put together. They were the perfect balance of slow songs and great dance tunes. She smiled as she thought about the special song that she had taped without Jed's knowledge. It had been one she and Jed had danced to on the night before graduation. That night had been wonderfully romantic, but Caitlin was sure that this night would be even more so as they danced beneath the full Montana moon.

As she stepped through the sliding glass door and onto the patio, she immediately began searching the sea of unfamiliar faces for Jed. She found him standing beside the barbecue pit, talking to a friend. She waited for a moment, hoping he'd turn to see how beautiful she looked framed in the doorway. She wanted to see him smile, then cross the patio and take her by the hand to introduce her to his friends.

But when he finally did turn around, a look of shock and embarrassment washed over his features. She saw him hesitate, almost as if he wished she would go back inside. A hush fell over the crowd, and everyone turned to stare at her. Uncomprehending, she glanced around. Only then did she notice what the other guests were wearing.

They were all in jeans. She was the only one who was dressed up.

Out of the corner of her eye, she caught sight of Melanie and Eve standing with two boys. Melanie was wearing her blue gingham shirt and jeans. Eve had on an emerald green western shirt with white piping and a pair of black jeans. Her hair was pulled back in a ponytail and held with a green ribbon that matched her shirt. In the quiet Caitlin heard her say to someone, "Well, doesn't she look just *too, too* pretty?" It was definitely a catty remark.

Jed, now halfway across the flagstone patio, said, "Not pretty—beautiful!" Reaching out his hand, he took Caitlin's and led her to the center of the crowd. "Everyone"—his voice was loud and clear—"this is Caitlin."

The group was still quiet. Then the silence was punctuated by a loud, masculine whistle. "Whoopee! Somebody book me on the next flight to Virginia. If the girls out there are like her, I want to be first in line."

The tension was broken. Everyone laughed and began milling about again. Some went over to say hello to Caitlin. Seeing that she was making friends, Jed excused himself and returned to his job overseeing the carving of the beef.

A pretty girl in a crisp red blouse and jeans was the first to speak. "Hi! I'm Lisa Brenner. I wanted to welcome you to Montana and tell you that I love what you're wearing. I think you look terrific." She leaned closer and said in a lower voice, "Don't pay any attention to Eve. She's just jealous. She's so used to being queen of this county that when someone like you shows up, she can't handle it."

"Yeah," the girl beside her agreed. "Lisa's right. And if you want to know the truth, I hope you've started a trend. We always wear jeans to parties, but I'd love to dress up once in a while." Suddenly, she realized she hadn't introduced herself. "Oh, by the way, I'm Sandy Craig."

"Hi, Sandy," Caitlin responded. "Hi, Lisa." She smiled warmly. "I'm really glad to meet you."

"Hey, how about me?" It was the guy who had broken the tension by whistling at her. He was now leaning over Sandy's shoulder.

"Oh, I suppose we can include you," Sandy said, moving so she could turn and link her arm through his. "This gorgeous guy is Colt Williams. Sometimes he lets me think he's my boyfriend, but I'm not always sure," she teased.

"What makes you say a thing like that?" Colt grinned down at her.

Sandy was about to answer him when Jed walked up to them, balancing two plates piled high with steaming barbecued beef, corn, and some dishes Caitlin didn't recognize. It smelled delicious. "Will you excuse us," Jed said. "Caitlin, I've got a place picked out for us over there." He pointed toward the far end of the patio. "You've really got to taste this sauce to believe it." He looked at the others. "Better get over there before it's all gone. Hank's still carving, but he won't be for long."

"Oh, boy! Lead me to it," Colt said. "Come on, gal," he told Sandy. "Let's go put on the feed bag."

"Colt! Be real!" Sandy glanced at Caitlin. "He doesn't usually talk this way, honest. It's all for your benefit."

"Why, Sandy, honey!" Colt looked astonished. "How can you fib like that to that nice lady? Your mama ought to wash your mouth out with soap."

Caitlin was laughing as they moved away. "Oh, Jed. Your friends are great. I really like them."

"Yeah, I like them, too. When I'm in Virginia, I really miss them a lot." He led her to a spot slightly away from the crowd. They sat down on a low stone wall beneath a string of lanterns, which swung gently in the evening breeze. The food was delicious, and hearty. To her surprise, Caitlin found she was really hungry. There was something about the open country air and spending her days working with Jed around the ranch that had almost doubled her already healthy appetite. But she hadn't gained weight, just a little more muscle.

She was thoroughly enjoying the delicious dinner when she looked up to see Eve coming toward them. Caitlin immediately lost her appetite. Eve was not alone. Melanie was with her, and so were the two boys she had seen with them earlier. The one who appeared to be with

Eve was dark and good-looking. Still, he was not nearly so handsome as Jed.

"Hi, there," Eve greeted them. "Great party, Jed." As they stopped in front of Jed and Caitlin, the dark-haired boy put his arm around Eve's waist. She leaned against him slightly. Caitlin wondered if she was trying to make Jed jealous. "We were just talking about the county fair and the horse race," Eve went on. "It's coming up pretty soon, you know. You never did say whether you would enter that four-legged joke of yours against Mr. Bars. Or maybe you're ready to admit right here and now that my horse is better than yours?"

"Oh, I don't think I have to prove anything, Eve." Jed shrugged. "I already know Charge Account is the best horse."

"But, does anyone else know that?" she asked to bait him.

"Who cares?"

"Oh, come on, Jed." The boy beside Melanie spoke up. "You know you do. And it would be great to see a race between a couple of horses who can really run. There hasn't been a good horse in that race since Charge Account's sire won it four years ago."

"Hey! Aren't you forgetting that Mr. Bars's dam won it the following year," Eve said hotly.

A few of the other guests, hearing them talk about the race, moved over to listen. A short, red-haired boy spoke up enthusiastically. "What do you say, Jed? This has all the makings of a great grudge match."

"Well—" Jed began to protest.

"Hey, yeah!" Another boy called from the back of the group. "Come on, Jed. Don't chicken out. The Michaels name is at stake here."

"Right!"

"Yeah!"

"Okay," Jed finally admitted, "I guess I'd like to. But Eve has an unfair advantage. She weighs about a hundred and five pounds. I weigh close to one-eighty."

"Well, guess that's that!" the last boy to speak said in defeat.

"Wait, just a second!" Eve held up her hand for silence. "I've got a great idea—one that would make the race fair." She pointed to Caitlin. "Caitlin can ride Charge Account." Her seemingly innocent turquoise eyes turned to meet Caitlin's blue ones. "How about it, Caitlin? Would you ride for Jed?"

"Oh, but I—" Caitlin stopped herself. She could see the challenge in Eve's eyes. *Well, why not?* she thought. She could ride rings around that jealous little pain in the neck. And she was almost as positive as Jed that his horse was the faster. Caitlin remembered that the fair would be held on the day before she and Jed were scheduled to fly back to Virginia. She liked thinking that Jed's last memory of their month in Montana would be of her beating Eve in a race on his horse.

"Okay, sure!" She smiled at Eve. "I'd love to win the race for Jed."

17

Caitlin decided not to mention to Melanie how angry she was about her trick since the party had been so successful. Also, Caitlin noticed that there was a difference in Melanie's attitude toward her—it was almost as if Jed's sister had come to like her. Melanie seemed to go out of her way to be nice to Caitlin, and Caitlin figured that Jed's sister must have seen how well she had gotten along with Jed's friends at the party and decided that she wasn't so bad after all.

So, as Caitlin sat curled up on the couch in the living room reading a book on the animals of the Rockies one evening, she wasn't surprised to have Melanie sit beside her.

The book she was reading was one she had found in the well-stocked shelves of the family room. She, Jed, Eve, and Melanie would be leaving the next morning for the three-day camping trip to Glacier Park that Jed had suggested, and Caitlin had decided to try to read up on the area. She wanted to learn enough so that she wouldn't say something stupid—something Eve could jump on.

As Melanie sat down, Caitlin held her place with her finger and flipped the book closed.

"Hi, Melanie. Are you all set for tomorrow?"

Melanie nodded. "Um-hmm. I've got my stuff all packed. Actually, that's why I came to find you. I wanted to see if you needed any help deciding what to take. I mean, after all, this is your first camping trip in the mountains, right?"

"Well, yes," Caitlin admitted. "And thanks for the offer. But Jed has already helped me decide what to take. And he found a pack for me." She smiled. "So I guess I'm all set, too."

"Great." Melanie nodded toward the book in Caitlin's hands. "Checking out where we're going?"

"Yes." Caitlin opened the book to show her the section she'd been glancing through.

"That's probably a good idea. It's pretty rugged country. And all those animals *are* out there. But"—she smiled with assurance—"Jed said you were a good shot. And we'll all be carrying rifles just in case." She tapped a page with a photograph of a snarling bear on it. "Boy, that's one animal I hope I never have to come face-to-face with. I'd wrestle with three mountain lions before I'd face one bear. A mountain lion will more than likely turn around and run. But a bear sometimes decides he simply doesn't like the way you look—and then watch out!" She pretended to shiver.

"Well, as you said, we'll have rifles," Caitlin

replied, putting on a show of confidence even though she was beginning to feel scared. It was all well and good to read about those fierce animals, but would she really know how to handle herself if she came face-to-face with one? And even though she did have a gun, shooting at a tin can was a lot different from shooting at some wild beast that was ready to kill.

"Actually," Melanie continued, pleased to see the fear on Caitlin's face, "I think I'm more afraid of some of the smaller animals—especially the ones that are poisonous." She rolled her eyes. "You can see mountain lions and bears before they come at you. But those little guys can hide in the brush right next to the path you're walking on, and before you know it—wham— they've bitten you. The next thing anyone knows, you're dead."

"Really?" Caitlin's apprehension was growing steadily.

"Yeah." Melanie nodded solemnly. "What's weird is that these animals are so adorable— almost cuddly. There's one." She pointed to a picture of a marmot. "See, it's got a bushy tail, and it looks like a woodchuck. But they're only distantly related. A marmot has these little poison sacks—back here." Melanie put her hands on either side of her own neck.

"Do you run across them very often?" Caitlin asked. She knew right then that it didn't matter what Melanie said, she herself simply wouldn't go walking on any paths where she might run into one.

"Oh, not really that often, I guess." Melanie shrugged. "They're mostly nocturnal. But all I can say is if you see an animal that looks like that, and it waddles, turn around and run the other way as fast as you can. Don't stop to look twice." She leaned forward, her eyes wide. "Because they're kind of like bears—they *attack*." At Melanie's final word, Caitlin jumped. Seeing this, Melanie shook her head. "But, don't worry, honestly. Jed'll be there to watch out for them. He knows his way around the mountains." She stood up. "Well, guess I'll turn in now. Since we're leaving so early tomorrow morning, I want to get some sleep."

"Yes, I think I will, too." Caitlin stood up, also. "I think I've had enough reading for tonight."

The interior of the cab was lit only by the dashboard lights. The darkness, along with the hypnotic hum of the engine, had lulled Caitlin back into a light sleep only minutes after Jed had pulled the truck and trailer out onto the main road. Since Melanie and Eve had decided to start the trip stretched out in sleeping bags in the horse trailer they were pulling, Caitlin had half of the wide front seat to herself.

Jed wanted to leave early because the trip north to the park near the Canadian border would take at least four hours. He also wanted to get there in plenty of time to take a long ride into the mountains. And before they could do anything else, they had to set up camp and give the horses time to get their "land legs" back after riding in the trailer for more than two hundred miles.

Caitlin awoke again after the sun had risen. It was shining on the truck and directly into her eyes. "Ummm." She stretched. "How long have we been driving, anyway?" she asked as she straightened out her legs and turned to look at Jed. "Aren't you tired? Would you like me to drive for a while?"

"No, thanks," Jed answered flatly. Then realizing how he had sounded, he quickly softened it by turning to give her a smile. "I'm fine."

The smile didn't fool Caitlin one bit. Something was wrong, and she knew it. But what? She noticed the tight set of the muscles in his jaw and the steely, hard look in his usually warm green eyes. "Jed, you can't fool me. I know something's wrong. Please don't keep it from me. We made a promise not to keep secrets, remember?"

"I remember."

"Well?"

"Okay, there is something that's bothering me," he said finally. "But I don't want to talk about it right now."

"Why? Now is the perfect time to talk about whatever's bothering you." She gestured with her hands. "I mean we've got loads of time. And there are just us two. Jed, I love you. Whatever it is, I want to help."

"You can't." Jed's voice was controlled, but it was forced.

"Try me!" Caitlin insisted.

For several long minutes, Jed did not speak. He continued to drive, looking straight ahead, concentrating on the road in front of them. Silently Caitlin waited for him to open up. Finally he did. And when he spoke, his voice was filled with pain. "My dad came into my room last night to have a talk with me. He's asked me to think about staying here—not going back to Virginia. He wants me to go to the same college he went to—because he wants me to come in with him and be his partner."

"What?" Caitlin didn't believe what she was hearing. "But I thought it was all decided. We're going to go to college together. Besides, you want to be a lawyer, not a rancher."

"I know!" Jed's voice was bitter. "But he's realized that he's getting older and can't manage the ranch alone."

"But that's nonsense!" Caitlin exploded. "He's not that old. I've watched him. He does the work of three men."

"I think his pride makes him act tougher than he is," Jed said. "I've been watching him when he didn't know I was looking, and I can see that he's slowed down. And I do understand how he feels. But—" Jed paused long enough to let out a long, sad sigh. "I've got my own life to consider as well. And you're right, I decided that I was going to go to school in Virginia and study prelaw. My dad even agreed." He glanced briefly at Caitlin, and she could see the misery in his eyes. "Now—now it's like none of it ever happened." Unhappiness showing in every line of his body, Jed returned to watching the road.

Caitlin sat still for several minutes while she mulled over what Jed had said. Then, in a quiet voice, she asked, "Didn't you say that he *asked* you to stay here. He didn't tell you you had to do it?"

Jed gave her an answering nod. "He left it up to me to make the decision."

"But, Jed, there's only one answer you can give," Caitlin insisted. "That's obvious."

"That's where you're wrong, Caitlin." Jed shook his head. "Maybe there is something to being a westerner after all. Last night my dad said the land was in my blood. He's right. I do love the ranch. And I love Montana." Jed was quiet for a moment before he said in a soft voice, "And I owe it to him."

"Oh, Jed." Caitlin was shaking her head. "You owe yourself something, too."

Jed didn't say anything. The silence in the cab grew more and more deafening. Caitlin couldn't stand it any longer. Finally she blurted out, almost angrily, "Is that your answer, then? You're going to give in to him? You're going to allow your father to dictate the rest of your life?"

"That's *not* what I said, Caitlin." Jed's voice matched hers in harsh intensity.

"Oh?" With a stricken feeling, Caitlin realized how thoughtlessly she had reacted. She wanted to take back the words she had flung at him.

Instead, she said softly, "Then you *haven't* made your decision yet?"

"No—no, I haven't." Jed's voice had softened, too. "There are still some things I have to weigh. I told him I'd give him an answer by the end of the week."

"I see."

They drove for another hour. Caitlin was so involved in her own thoughts that she hardly noticed their leaving the rolling grassland behind and the road becoming shaded by a band of spruce and aspen. Then they emerged into a natural meadow, which surrounded a clear alpine lake. Sheer granite mountains rose up all around them. It was only as Jed pulled the pickup into the parking area that she realized they had arrived.

Automatically she got out of the truck and went through the motions of helping to unload the horses, tethering them to the side of the trailer, then taking a bucket down to the lake to get water for them.

Eve and Melanie stepped out of the trailer and started unloading some of the gear that had been packed in the bed of the truck. As they carried the camping equipment to the site Jed had picked out, Caitlin continued to bring water to the horses and walk each one in turn so it wouldn't stiffen up.

As she finished refastening the lead of the last horse to the side of the trailer, Caitlin was still too upset to join the others immediately. She decided to take a short walk instead, completely forgetting that she had promised herself she wouldn't walk on narrow paths alone.

She had gone only about fifty feet when she heard footsteps behind her. "Caitlin! Caitlin, wait." Stopping, she turned around and saw that it was Melanie. "Where do you think you're going by yourself?" Melanie asked as she came up beside Caitlin. "You could get lost, or— *whatever*." She emphasized the word "whatever" to allow it to work on Caitlin's imagination.

"I wasn't going very far," Caitlin replied. "And I promise I won't leave this path. It seems pretty well worn."

"At least take a rifle." Melanie held the gun out. "It'll make me feel better if I know you have it with you."

"Okay," Caitlin agreed wearily. She accepted the gun. "I won't be gone long."

"Good." Melanie seemed satisfied. She smiled. "Enjoy yourself."

As Melanie started back toward the campsite, Caitlin transferred the gun to her right hand so she could carry it loosely in the crook of her arm as Jed had taught her. The muzzle was pointing down so that she couldn't accidentally shoot someone, but also so that it would be ready to be raised and fired. She started forward again. The path she was on was very narrow, and meandered through the brush and trees. It appeared to have been made by some sort of animal—a deer, perhaps.

She had been walking for a few minutes when

she paused to look up at a bird in a nearby tree. As she stood there, she heard some rustling in the nearby brush. Her heart began to pound as she recalled pictures of mountain lions and bears.

She was relieved when, instead of the ferocious creatures she had been envisioning, a short, furry animal waddled out onto the path some five feet in front of her. She let out the breath she had been holding and laughed at her own foolishness.

The little animal, surprised at the sound, stopped in its tracks and turned its head swiftly to see where the unexpected sound was coming from.

Seeing the tiny face looking at her, the laughter died in her throat. It was a marmot—a very cute, very poisonous marmot. She stood absolutely still, thinking that if she didn't move or make another sound, the creature might go away.

The animal hesitated as they stared at each other. Then the marmot started toward her. Perhaps, as Caitlin thought about it later, it had only been about to turn and go in the opposite direction. But at that moment it seemed to her that the animal had been about to attack. Instinctively, she raised the rifle and shot.

A bullet cracked from the gun, and almost at the exact same instant, a blotch of red appeared against the light brown fur. The little animal looked up at Caitlin with soft, frightened eyes.

Then, as she watched, its eyes slowly glazed over, and the animal collapsed into a pitiful heap.

Caitlin stood there in shock. She had never killed anything before. All at once, the realization of what she had done washed over her, leaving her knees shaking.

She was still standing rooted to the spot, unable to take her eyes from the tiny dead animal, when she heard the sound of feet pounding up behind her.

"Caitlin! Caitlin!" Jed was calling. "Are you all right? Answer me, Caitlin!" Then he was beside her. She heard him draw a sharp breath as he, too, saw the dead animal. "Oh, no!" he exclaimed.

"Yes—I know," Caitlin finally managed to get out. "It was a close call."

"Close call!" Jed's voice sounded shocked. "What are you talking about, Caitlin? How could that innocent little marmot hurt you?" Reaching over, he took the rifle firmly away from her.

She turned to look into Jed's horror-filled eyes. "But—but that's a poisonous—" She stopped talking. Looking past Jed's shoulder, she saw Eve look at Melanie with a satisfied expression on her face. As though someone had just dumped a glass of ice water on her, she realized what had happened. She had been set up once again to look bad in Jed's eyes. And the setup had succeeded perfectly! But even worse, she had killed a perfectly defenseless animal.

"Oh, Jed." She started to move toward him, wanting to throw herself into his arms so she could be comforted. "I feel absolutely awful about this."

Jed almost jumped away from her in his effort to keep her from touching him. Looking at her coldly, he said in a low tone, "So do I, Caitlin. So do I."

18

A couple of days later Melanie and Eve were sitting in the sun on a stack of hay bales piled beside the Michaelses' stable.

"I'd have been willing to bet almost anything that Caitlin Ryan would have been gone by now." Pulling a piece of hay from a bale, Eve toyed with it thoughtfully. "That stunt with the marmot should've done it. And Jed certainly looked angry enough. I've never been on such a short camping trip in my life."

"I have to agree with you there." Melanie paused to grin. "Two hours is the shortest camping trip I've ever been on, too."

Eve grinned back at her. "I wish I had a picture of Caitlin's face when she found out that that animal she'd just shot was perfectly harmless."

"Me, too!" Melanie agreed and tried to laugh. But her laughter died in her throat. Now that Eve had reminded her, the picture of the dead animal came back to her. It made her feel ashamed of the part she had played in the animal's death. "I do feel kind of bad about that poor little thing, though," she admitted. "It looked so pitiful, lying there."

"Oh, Melanie, stop it!" Eve sounded annoyed. "You're responsible for animals dying all the time. What do you think happens to all the cattle that get shipped off to the market? And all those cute little calves. You don't think people buy them as pets, do you?"

"That's different," Melanie insisted.

"How? Because you don't see them get killed? Believe me, dead is dead." She shook her head. "But I don't want to talk about that. I want to talk about Jed." She squinted. "What I can't figure out is that one minute he was so upset about what Caitlin did that we packed up and came right home. But now he's being nice to her again. How come? Do you think she told him what you told her about the marmot?"

"No, she's been quiet about all our tricks. She hasn't told Jed, I'm sure. Guess she figures it's just between us. I don't know if I'm right about this," Melanie said. "But I might have an idea."

"You do?" Eve leaned forward. "Well, tell me, for heaven's sake," she said impatiently.

"Okay, okay. I think it's like this. When we started out on this trip, Jed was already unhappy. But we didn't notice it because we were back in the trailer the whole time."

"What was he upset about?"

"My dad finally got around to talking to Jed about staying here and going to Montana Agricultural College instead of going to that college in the East. He did it the night before we left.

Also, I know that he told Jed he didn't approve of Caitlin because he doesn't think she fits in here. So, when Caitin shot that innocent animal, it just kind of proved what my father had said was right."

"But that's absolutely great!" Eve exclaimed. "Melanie, that's exactly what we've been working toward, right? Funny how your father's on our side, even though he doesn't know it." She smiled to herself. "Jed was just upset because our trick finally made him realize that she doesn't fit in. It bothered him for a while, but he's over that now. And he's just being polite to her because there are only a few days left before she flies home to Virginia. I guess he feels he has to be nice. That's just the way Jed is." Crossing her arms, she hugged herself. "Now I can really start planning. Just think, Jed and I will be spending the whole year at school together— two little freshmen at Montana Agricultural College. I've got to—"

"Hold it!" Melanie interrupted Eve's happy chatter. "You didn't let me finish."

"Finish?" Eve scowled. "Finish what?"

"What I was saying. Look, Jed hasn't agreed to stay here yet. He said he'd think about it, that's all. And saying you'll think about something is a lot different from giving a definite yes. Jed could still be planning to fly back to Virginia with Caitlin on Sunday. You wouldn't see him again for another year. They could even be married by then."

"Don't be stupid, Melanie," Eve snapped.

161

"Jed's not going to marry anyone until he graduates from college."

Melanie shrugged. "You never know."

"Oh, just shut up for a second and let me think."

Melanie was quiet, pulling out a length of hay and chewing on it while she watched Eve consider the situation.

"I've got it!" Eve said several minutes later. "We just have to pull one more little trick on Caitlin—one so terrible that it will convince both her and Jed that they aren't right for each other."

"I'm almost afraid to ask," Melanie said. "What are you planning? And if it involves anyone getting hurt, don't tell me. That animal was enough for me." She looked at her friend curiously. "You know, Eve, sometimes you do scare me."

"Oh, Melanie." Eve rolled her eyes. "Nobody's going to get hurt. Maybe knocked around a little, but definitely not hurt."

"Now I know I don't want to hear it." Melanie put her hands over her ears and shut her eyes.

Eve waited patiently until Melanie lowered her hands and opened one eye. "Come on, Melanie. We've come this far together. Don't chicken out now. I promise you, Caitlin will fly home in one piece. But by the time she leaves, she'll never want to come west again."

"Oh, all right, tell me," Melanie agreed warily. "But why do I think I'm going to regret this?"

"Only if you screw up. Which you won't, because I'm going to do most of the work. You just have to make sure that Caitlin doesn't discover what I've done."

"No, don't tell me." Melanie started to put her hands over her ears again, then lowered them when Eve gave her a stern look. "Okay, what is it?"

"It's so great because this way I'll be sure to win the race on Saturday at the fair. Here's my plan: I'm going to fix Charge Account's saddle so it'll start getting loose right at the start. That will throw her riding off just enough so that she won't be able to control him, and he'll go dashing all over the place. She'll look like a total jerk. In the end, Caitlin will be one huge failure in Jed's eyes. Especially when I cross the finish line and win the trophy."

"How are you going to do that? Whatever you do, Caitlin's sure to spot it."

"Not if you keep her distracted. You see, I'm going to weaken the cinch on one side. When she goes to saddle Count, you be there to help her so that she doesn't have to go around and check the other side. Very few people check that side of the saddle when they're tacking up, anyway. They get lazy."

"Not Caitlin." Melanie shook her head. "She's a very careful rider."

"Well, just make sure she's *not* a careful rider on Saturday."

The wonderful smells and sounds of the fair reached Caitlin as she stood grooming Count one last time before the race. She was purposely ignoring them, concentrating only on running the brush over his already glistening palomino coat. She was checking for any small cuts or bumps he might have sustained during the ride from the ranch in the trailer. She was also trying to think ahead to how the powerfully muscled gelding would react to the crowd and to the other horses. She had been riding Count a lot in the past few days, and she knew he had the speed and the stamina to be a winner. But, as Jed had told her, he had never been in a race before, even one as casual as the one that afternoon.

Jed had left five minutes earlier to check on the entry procedure, and she was alone for the moment. Thinking of Jed, she thanked God he was no longer angry with her. Killing the poor little animal had been an accident, a terrible, carefully planned accident. But Jed didn't know the truth. Caitlin had told him that she thought she had remembered reading somewhere that marmots really were poisonous. There was no way she was going to tell him that Eve, along with Melanie, had planned the entire tragic incident. That would only make matters worse. It would reduce Caitlin to the level of telling tales in Jed's eyes.

She was glad that the next day they would be on a plane flying back to Virginia. She paused, the brush against Count's neck. But what if Jed didn't fly back with her? The thought made her stomach lurch. She knew he still hadn't decided. The night before, when they had gone for a walk, he'd told her he hadn't.

"Thinking about the race?"

Caitlin jumped with surprise at the sound of Melanie's voice. She glanced over to see Jed's sister leaning against the side of the trailer, only a few feet away.

"Hello, Melanie," Caitlin said in a cold voice. "How long have you been standing there?"

"Just a few minutes. I didn't say anything at first because you looked so deep in thought."

"What are you doing here?" Caitlin asked.

"Oh, Eve's acting all uptight about Mr. Bars. You know, getting him ready. I got tired of hanging around her, so I came over to see how you were doing."

You mean to spy, don't you, Caitlin thought to herself. Aloud, she said, "Hand me that hoof pick, will you? It's right beside you in the tack box."

Melanie reached down, got the tool Caitlin had asked for, and handed it to her. She took the body brush in return and put it back in the box. "Where's Jed?"

"He went to check on the race procedures," Caitlin said. Grunting slightly, she bent and lifted one of Count's feet, resting it against her leg so she could remove any small obstacle, such as a pebble, that might have gotten caught in the sensitive area.

She went on to check Count's three other hooves. As she handed Melanie the pick, she glanced at her watch. "Looks like it's time to tack up. The race starts in fifteen minutes.

Reaching for the saddle pad and blanket, she

put them on first, making sure the hair beneath them was lying smoothly and all in the same direction. Then, grabbing the saddle by the horn, she lifted it and swung it over Count's back. She settled it snugly into the slight dip just behind his withers. Then she bent and reached under his belly to grab the cinch so she could bring it up and fasten it with the latigo strap that was attached to her side of the saddle. Melanie was standing on the opposite side, and she quickly bent and passed it to Caitlin.

"Thanks," Caitlin said, running the long leather strap through the metal ring sewn to the end of the stringed, mohair cinch. Pulling it up, she threaded it through three times and then knotted it at the top, almost the way a man would knot a tie. She left it fairly loose for a moment, intending to tighten it more just before mounting.

"Almost ready?" Jed came up as she was undoing the halter and sliding Count's bridle up over his head.

"Yes. All set," she answered, checking briefly to see that the bit was lying correctly in the horse's mouth.

"Well, I guess I'll go over and find a place to sit in the stands," Melanie said. "Good luck, Caitlin."

"Did you wish Eve luck as well?"

"Of course. I wish everyone luck." Melanie smiled pleasantly, then turned to walk away.

"What was that all about?" Jed asked. "You two don't seem to be acting very friendly toward each other today."

"It's nothing. She came over to say hello and see if I was nervous, that's all."

"And are you?"

"No." She smiled at Jed as she gave Count a pat on the neck. "We plan on winning, don't we, boy?" she said to the horse.

"Well, then, let's go." Jed stepped over, tightened the cinch for her, then helped her up.

He walked with her as far as the starting line, where about fifteen other riders were already waiting. Eve was there, mounted on the dark chestnut, Mr. Bars. She saw them. Raising a hand, she waved gaily in their direction. Jed waved back. Caitlin made a pretense of brushing something from the leg of her jeans so she wouldn't have to wave.

Jed turned and put one hand on Count's withers, the other over the hand Caitlin was resting lightly on top of the horn. "I know you two are going to run a terrific race," he told her in a low, tender voice. "And even though I'll be up in the stands with Dad, I'll be with you in spirit." His hand squeezed hers. "Win or lose, though, you'll always be a winner to me."

"Thank you, Jed," Caitlin replied softly, looking into his intense green eyes. What she saw was the message that, despite anything that might happen now, or in the future, he would always love her.

"Well," Jed said, stepping back, "guess I'd better get out of the way. But as I said, I'll be up there in the stands, cheering you all the way."

Caitlin continued to watch Jed as he moved

with long, strong strides toward the bleachers. Then she turned Charge Account and guided him into line. Eve was only five horses away from her. She looked very calm, giving no hint of the nervousness Melanie had mentioned to Caitlin. In fact, she seemed extremely self-assured.

The starter began walking down the line, making sure all the horses were lined up evenly. As he passed in front of the horse beside Count, he accidentally brushed the horse's nose with his hand. The horse reacted by snorting and backing quickly. This, in turn, startled Count, and he gave a little crow-hop. The small movement surprised Caitlin, but she placed a hand on his neck, saying in a soothing tone, "Easy, boy. Easy." But Count gave one more small buck before he settled down.

As he did, Caitlin felt the saddle slip slightly. Not really alarmed, she leaned over to check the latigo leather holding the cinch in place. It was fine. But the saddle seemed to be loosening even more. Holding Count's reins tightly so that he couldn't jump foward, she leaned to the right. She now realized what was happening. The mohair strands of the cinch were popping, one at a time. In another second they would all go, leaving the saddle completely unsecured.

She heard the starter asking if everyone was ready, and she started to raise her hand to indicate that she wasn't. But before she could, he yelled, "Go!" The horses on either side of Caitlin took off. Caitlin could feel Count's muscles bunching beneath her. He, too, wanted to run. It took all of Caitlin's strength to pull back on the reins to keep Count from following the other horses. He reared as she tried to restrain him, and the saddle slid down and landed on the ground. There was nothing Caitlin could do but slide with it. Fortunately, she had kicked her feet out of the stirrups, jumping at the last minute to land on her feet. She was even able to hold on to one of the reins.

The saddle was now lying in a heap to one side, while Count plunged nervously about at the end of the single rein. A girl up in the stands screamed, and a man yelled, "Someone, help that girl!"

Caitlin, however, didn't need any help. She had the situation well in hand. Pulling the horse closer to her, she talked to him in soothing tones and immediately calmed him, then reached over and grabbed the other rein, and pulled the two together at the top of his withers. Then she swung herself up onto his back in one easy motion.

Caitlin turned the horse and nudged him with her heels. He didn't need a second cue. With a tremendous leap forward, he was immediately pounding down the track, trying to catch up to the other horses. As she felt Count's muscles bunch and reach, bunch and reach, she realized that with the heavy saddle gone, she had a definite advantage over the other riders. It was almost as though she were riding English. She had the same freedom the smaller saddle afforded. Not only that, but Count wasn't carrying as much weight.

They were catching up quickly. As they approached the other riders, however, Caitlin could see she had a problem. The pack was so tightly grouped together that it didn't look as though they would be able to find a place to slip past the leaders. The finish line was coming up fast. She had to decide instantly whether to wait for an opening or take a chance and go around. Caitlin wondered if Count still had enough energy to make it around, or if he had used it all up in his almost miraculous charge to catch up to the others. Then, Count seemed to make the decision for her. He broke to the right, and she knew immediately that he wanted to win the race as much as she did. Giving him his head, she leaned over his neck and whispered, "Go, Count. Go!"

He charged forward with such a burst of speed that they were soon passing even the leaders. But Eve was out in front alone. As Caitlin drew up next to her, Eve glanced over. She had such a look of shock on her face when she realized it was Caitlin that Caitlin was afraid for a moment that Eve might faint and fall off her horse. But Eve managed to get hold of herself. "*Damn* you, Caitlin Ryan," she called.

With an expression of grim determination, she began slapping the ends of the reins back and forth across her horse's shoulders in an attempt to make him go faster. But it was useless. Mr. Bars was already winded, while Charge Account seemed as fresh as though he were out for a lazy canter. He pulled ahead, and he and Caitlin crossed the finish line with two lengths to spare.

The crowd went crazy as Caitlin brought Count down to a prancing walk. Raising a hand as she came back in front of the grandstand, she waved at the standing ovation they were giving her. Then she saw Jed leap over the bleacher railing and come running toward her. Several feet from her, he slowed to avoid frightening Count. Jed walked up to them and put both hands on Count's shoulder as if to steady himself. Caitlin noticed his hands were shaking slightly. "God. Oh, God, Caitlin . . ." He shook his head from side to side and then looked up into her eyes. "I thought for a moment that you were going to be killed out there. Then you came through like nothing I've ever seen. And, on top of that, you won!"

"Hey, you two!" An official came over, grinning as he did. "Don't just stand there. Everyone's waiting for you to come over to the judge's stand and accept your trophy."

"I'm going to go get that saddle," Jed said a short time later as they walked toward the trailer. Caitlin was carrying the trophy, as well as leading Count. "I want to see exactly what happened to make it come off like that."

"I'd like to know, too," Caitlin agreed. "Right now, though, I'm going to take Count to the trailer and give him a good rubdown. He deserves it."

Caitlin had just finished brushing the horse and had put a blanket over him when Jed came storming up to the trailer. The saddle was flung over one shoulder. When he reached her, he threw it down on the ground with disgust. Flipping back the leather that normally covered the cinch, he said furiously, "There's the reason the saddle came off! The cinch wore out and snapped."

"Wh-what do you mean?" Caitlin could not believe what she was hearing. "But how can that be? I checked the entire saddle out this morning."

Jed knew Caitlin was a careful rider. She would never have put a saddle on a horse without checking it thoroughly. "Then someone must have cut it. And they did it so it would look as though the cinch had simply worn out." Jed shook his head. "It had to have been one of the other contestants, but who?" He stood there, looking like an angry bull. "It was a friendly race! There wasn't anything to gain by winning but a silly trophy. And by rigging your saddle, they put you in terrible danger. I just don't understand."

But Caitlin did. With a sick feeling, she realized why the cinch had been cut and who had done it. As she stood there trying to think what would be the best way to handle the situation, Melanie came running up to them. Her face was pale. She looked first at the saddle, then at Jed and Caitlin. Caitlin could have sworn she turned even whiter, if that was possible. "Oh, Caitlin! Am I ever glad you're all right."

"Yes," Caitlin answered, looking coolly back at the girl. "I'm fine. Thanks for your concern."

"When I saw what happened I got so scared. I thought you were going to be hurt or killed."

"She almost was," Jed said. The anger he felt still showed in his voice. "But, listen, Melanie, now that you're here, would you stay with Caitlin? I want to go tell Dad about this."

"D-Dad?" Melanie's voice choked. Caitlin thought she looked as if she were going to faint.

"Yeah." Jed nodded. "I think the saddle was tampered with deliberately so that it would come off during the race."

"Tampered with?" Melanie asked.

"Yes." Caitlin suddenly felt pity for Melanie. "But we don't know who." She turned to Jed. "Jed, I don't think it's really necessary to find out who did it. They're probably almost as upset about what they've done as you are. I don't think whoever it was meant to really hurt me. They probably just wanted the saddle to slip enough so I'd lose the race." She touched his arm to soothe him. "Please, forget about it. I don't want to leave Montana with people disliking me for causing problems."

"But, Caitlin—" Jed started to protest. Then shaking his head, he agreed. "All right. Knowing you, I guess I understand. But someday, I promise you, I'll find out—if only for myself." He turned. "I still have to go talk to my dad, to let him know you're really okay. He asked me to make sure. Melanie—"

"I'll stay here, Jed," Melanie promised.

Both Caitlin and Melanie watched as Jed walked away.

"You know, don't you?" Melanie spoke first.

"I guessed."

"I'm sorry, Caitlin." Melanie looked pleadingly at her. "I know that doesn't even begin to make up for what I did. But when I saw how awful Eve's trick turned out, I realized I couldn't let things go on. I had to come and tell you—to warn you before she pulled anything else." Suddenly her shoulders began to shake, and she covered her face. "Oh, Caitlin," she said, sobbing. "I really am sorry. Really."

"Eve planned this?"

"But I helped!" Melanie uncovered her face. Her eyes were red, and her cheeks were stained with tears. But her voice was steady as she said, "I'm just as responsible as Eve is. She frayed the cinch, but I was here to make sure you didn't notice."

"Oh, Melanie." Caitlin sighed unhappily.

"But Eve promised that nothing bad would happen to you. She said all that would happen would be that your saddle would become loose and you'd lose the race. Honest!"

Melanie looked so miserable that Caitlin was beginning to feel some sympathy for her. "I guess I believe you, Melanie. It's just that I still can't quite understand why you hate me enough to do this." She closed her eyes and shook her head. "I can understand Eve's hating me—but not you."

"But I don't hate you," Melanie cried out. "I

really like you. And I admire you, too. You didn't tell on us when we pulled all those tricks. But, well, no one tells Eve not to do something. And she is my best friend." Melanie stopped talking and looked helplessly at Caitlin.

"I guess I just wanted us to be friends as well," Caitlin said softly.

"Do—do you think we still could be friends?"

"I'd like that," Caitlin said at last.

Melanie gave a happy sigh. "Oh, Caitlin, thank you. I'm so glad you understand." She smiled. "I really am." Suddenly her smile turned to a look of fear. "What about the saddle? What if Jed finds out that I had a part in almost getting you killed? He'll hate me forever."

"Don't worry, Melanie," Caitlin assured her. "I promise you, I'll never tell. Only you and I and Eve will ever know the real truth."

"Oh, thank you, Caitlin."

"We're friends." Caitlin smiled. "Remember?"

But she was certainly not friends with Eve, she told herself. Caitlin marched furiously over to Eve's horse trailer.

Eve had just finished loading Mr. Bars and was facing the trailer to lock it as Caitlin walked up.

"Excuse me, Eve. I'd like to speak to you for a moment." Caitlin's voice was cold and business-like.

Hearing her, Eve gave a startled little jump before turning to face her. She gave Caitlin a weak smile. "Sure. What is it? By the way, I'm sorry you had that problem with your saddle. I guess you didn't check it very well before you got on. You know you really should be more careful." She shrugged. "And here I thought you were supposed to be such a great little horsewoman."

"I am a good horsewoman," Caitlin replied in a tone as icy as the look in her eyes. "Enough to know when a piece of equipment has been deliberately tampered with. Even if I hadn't already been told."

"Melanie told—" Too late, Eve realized she had given herself away. There was no use protesting any further. Narrowing her eyes, she glared at Caitlin. "Well, so what. I'm glad you know." She glanced uneasily around. "But you still can't pin it on me. I don't care what Melanie said."

"I don't intend to say anything. I've already made my peace with Jed's sister. But as for you, I just wanted to tell you, face to face, what a rotten person I think you are. And if you know what's good for you, you'll never think of pulling a stunt like that again. Because I'll know about it. And next time I won't stop at just a warning."

"Oh?" One corner of Eve's mouth lifted in a sarcastic sneer. "Really?"

"Yes," Caitlin spat out. "Really!" With that, she turned on her heel and strode away.

19

Jed and Caitlin spent the rest of the afternoon walking around, enjoying the fair. It was Caitlin's first one, and she wanted to do everything, from eating greasy tacos and drinking pink lemonade to riding the Ferris wheel, which they did five times. Jed even threatened to win her a huge stuffed panda, but she managed to convince him she didn't really want one.

It was dark by the time they got home. They stabled Count, and Caitlin insisted that Jed give him an extra measure of oats for having won the race in spite of everything. She also did it because it would be the last time she would see the horse until perhaps the next summer.

After giving Count a final pat on the neck, Caitlin and Jed walked out of the barn. The moon, although not so full as it had been the night of the party, was still bright. It turned the night into a beautiful landscape of silver and black. Jed stopped her beside a corral. Leaning against it, he took her hands in his and held them between his two strong ones. He continued to stand there, saying nothing for such a long time that Caitlin began to feel frightened. "Jed," she said softly, "what is it? Why are you so sad?" She was afraid she knew what his answer would be.

As an answer, Jed sighed heavily and squeezed her hands even tighter.

"Jed!"

"Caitlin—" His voice was hoarse with emotion. "Caitlin, I won't be going back with you tomorrow. I've made my decision. I'm going to stay here. I'm going to go to Montana Agricultural College, at least for this year."

"No!" Caitlin's cry was anguished. "Say you don't mean that!"

"I'm sorry, but I have to stay."

"But you can't!" Caitlin's voice was almost a wail. "I need you. You have to come back with me." Even as she went on, she knew she was being selfish. But she couldn't help it. She needed Jed—she needed his help. "I've got all these problems to face. Nicole's trying to wrap my father around her little finger. And there's Colin. I don't know what he's up to, but I know that it's no good."

"Caitlin." Jed had released her hands and was now cupping his hands about her shoulders in a comforting manner. "I know you better than that. You're strong. You don't need me there in order to cope with either Nicole or Colin. You'd handle those problems whether I was there or not."

"I suppose you're right," Caitlin admitted. Jed's reasoning had gotten through to her. She knew he was right and that her outburst had been born out of selfishness, out of the fear that she might be losing him forever. She looked up into his face, seeing his strong, handsome features sharply defined in the bright moonlight. "It's that I hate the thought of not being with you. . . ." She couldn't finish

"I know." Jed's eyes were echoing the pain she was feeling. "I can't bear the thought of not seeing *you* every day. But I'll be thinking about you. I promise you that. There won't be a day that goes by when I won't picture you walking across the campus, the wind blowing in your hair—or studying in your dorm room late at night." He smiled sweetly. "We'll just have to be together in spirit."

"Oh, Jed, I love you so very much."

"And I love you," Jed answered. Slipping his hands from her shoulders to her back, he pulled her gently to him, kissing her tenderly, first on the neck, then on her mouth. As he did, a slight shudder ran through him. He tightened his embrace, and his lips became more insistent, almost bruising in their passion. Caitlin found herself answering his kisses completely. When they finally parted, Caitlin leaned her head against his chest. She let out a long sigh as Jed's arms continued to hold her protectively to him.

* * *

It was with the remembrance of that final embrace that Jed watched Caitlin's plane lift up from the runway, bank, and grow smaller as it flew eastward.

At that very moment, some two thousand miles away, someone else was thinking about Caitlin Ryan, making plans that would involve her in the coming year. Kathy Stokes's brother was standing in the doorway of his parents' cabin. He was holding a medical book in his hand. Slowly he opened it to reveal a clipping taken from the society pages of the *Middletown Courier*. The clipping was a photo of Caitlin, taken earlier in the summer. It was an announcement of her enrollment as a freshman at Carleton Hill University. It was just what he needed to set his revenge in motion. He smiled grimly.

In the plane Caitlin unbuckled her seat belt after getting airborne. She had watched Jed as he stood beside the pickup near the terminal building for as long as she could. But the plane had made a turn, banking so that the wing obscured her view. Now she knew she must turn her thoughts ahead, to what lay before her in Virginia. It would be an exciting year at college. And she would be seeing her father again. Nicole would still be there, but Caitlin knew that somehow she would handle the situation. And Colin, too. She did wish that Jed would be with her. But, as he had said, he would be there in spirit. She would hold on to that thought.

Settling back against her seat, Caitlin closed her eyes. For now, she would remember again all the wonderful details of their time alone the night before.

FRANCINE PASCAL

In addition to collaborating on the Broadway musical *George M!* and the nonfiction book *The Strange Case of Patty Hearst*, Francine Pascal has written an adult novel, *Save Johanna!*, and four young adult novels, *Hangin' Out with Cici*, *My First Love and Other Disasters*, *The Hand-Me-Down Kid*, and *Love and Betrayal & Hold the Mayo!* She is also the creator of the Sweet Valley High series. Ms. Pascal has three daughters, Jamie, Susan, and Laurie, and lives in New York City.

DIANA GREGORY

Growing up in Hollywood, Diana Gregory wanted to become an actress. She became an associate TV producer instead. Now a full-time writer, she has written, in addition to other books, three young adult novels, *I'm Boo! That's Who!*, *There's a Caterpillar in My Lemonade*, and *The Fog Burns Off by Eleven O'clock*, plus several Sweet Dreams novels. Besides writing, her other love is traveling. She has lived in several states, including Virginia, where she stayed on a horse farm for a year. She now calls Seattle home.

Celebrate the Seasons
with SWEET VALLEY HIGH
Super Editions

Now you can join the Gang in

WINTER CARNIVAL
The New SWEET VALLEY HIGH Super Edition

You've been a SWEET VALLEY HIGH fan all along—hanging out with Jessica and Elizabeth and their friends at Sweet Valley High. And now the SWEET VALLEY HIGH *Super Editions* give you more of what you like best—more romance—more excitement—more real-life adventure! Whether you're bicycling up the California Coast in PERFECT SUMMER, dancing at the Sweet Valley Christmas Ball in SPECIAL CHRISTMAS, touring the South of France in SPRING BREAK, catching the rays in a MALIBU SUMMER, or skiing the snowy slopes in WINTER CARNIVAL—you know you're exactly where you want to be—with the gang from SWEET VALLEY HIGH.

SWEET VALLEY HIGH SUPER EDITIONS

☐ PERFECT SUMMER
25072/$2.95
☐ SPRING BREAK
25537/$2.95

☐ SPECIAL CHRISTMAS
25377/$2.95
☐ MALIBU SUMMER
26050/$2.95

Prices and availability subject to change without notice.

and watch for
WINTER CARNIVAL
Coming soon!